Dragon Silver, Wizard Gold

Book 1 in The Varthien Saga

Dragon Silver, Wizard Gold

Kris Sihto

Kris Sihto
2025

First Published: 2024

2nd Edition 2025

Paperback ISBN 978-0-9942984-3-0
eBook ISBN 978-0-9942984-4-7

Cover Art *Peter and Petunia* ©2012 Kris Sihto

Acknowledgements

This book could not have come together without the help of many wonderful people who I would like to thank.

Colleen Facey, you helped me get past the 10,000 word mark. Without your encouragement, this book might never have been started.

Thank you, Bruce Kinghorn, for encouraging me to continue to write "even to the detriment of all else", for driving me to and from our Writing Fridays group, and for being my sounding board on all things bookish. I know it was a little disjointed for you reading so many things out of sequence, but you persevered. Your editing tips and questions were essential.

Thank you, Des, for your early feedback about Norman. His story is an important one and I am glad you could be the first to hear it. Going on to read for me throughout the rest of the book pushed me to write faster — I loved seeing your excitement as the story unfolded for you.

T. K. Sihto, your reactions to some of the moments in my chapters helped me understand how I had fared with emotional impact.

Crispian Kinghorn and Lukasz Gogolkiewicz, I reached out to you both to understand some of Peter's childhood motivations. You helped me build a more faceted personality for this very pivotal character. Thank you.

And Philomena Boman, thank you for being an ear for so long.

Introduction

661 OM Tarandeer
Year of the Tangled Briar

Norman's Tower

A loud rumble shook the room, and Peter opened an eye. The liquid in the potion bottles, which were neatly lined up in the cabinet across from him, danced in multi-hued sloshes. Dust sifted down from the stones above. He snuggled further into the warm cocoon of blankets to escape the trickle of grit.

Peter's eye closed again, but part of him waited for the inevitable banging and swearing that always followed incidents like this.

...

...

...

...

After what seemed an eternity, but was perhaps less than five minutes, Peter sighed and rolled out of his narrow bed. He cringed slightly at the cold stone on his bare feet, then braved the chill of the air to run for the robe he had dumped carelessly in the corner. The coals had long since died in the fireplace, and the air felt like icicles against his skin. He was shivering violently by the time he managed to sort the neck out from the armholes and cursing under his breath at the ineptitude of wizards, particularly those named Norman.

"...What sort of a name is 'Norman' for a wizard anyway?" he asked the silence, as he slipped his feet into thin, cloth slippers.

The silence mocked him severely by remaining silent.

He set his feet to the bottom step and started the ascent, cursing for the millionth time the cheapness of the wizard whose tower consisted of three rooms, the bottom of which happened to hold the numerous functions of entrance foyer, storage closet, kitchen, and Peter's bedroom, and whose tower stairs worked in the mundane fashion.

The middle storey appeared in the dimness to be as always, a dining table lying hidden beneath piles of books and scrolls, more potions, and that ever-present fungus which seemed to be growing from the wood (Peter had tried to scrub it out, but everything he did just seemed to make it grow faster). An old, tin bathtub sat forlornly across the room, under the window with the extensive water pulley system Peter had built some years ago to end the torturous carrying back and forth.

He eyed the thin beam of red light that shone from above — just a crack from the doorway — and hesitantly started up the last flight. Norman didn't like to be disturbed, but silence was never a good thing to hear after one of Norman's "accidents". The wizard could be lying unconscious, or even (Peter's mind barely dared to think it) dead.

The air was warmer here, and as his hand reached for the door handle it felt like it had been bathed in summer sun. The brass handle was hot to the touch, and horrid imagined scenes flitted through his mind of scorched flesh.

He turned the handle and entered the room.

Chapter 1

653 OM Tarandeer
Year of the Leaping Rabbit

Pugton

The boy squelched chilly mud through his toes as he squatted between two market stalls. The hustle and bustle of the market went unheard, his concentration unwavering as he gazed in rapt fascination at the earthworm between his feet. It writhed wildly, covered in the thick mud.

He had been inspecting the worm for some time now, and it was starting to slow. Suddenly he started wondering why it was the worm was flailing about in the first place. Did worms like to flail about? He imagined that their lives underground were fairly boring really.

And then it hit him. It had been raining steadily through the night, and everything was waterlogged. He wondered what it would be like if he were only the size of the worm before him, trapped in sticky mud as far as he could see and unable to get out.

With a grimy finger, he reached out and gently smoothed some of the mud from the skin of the worm.

"There, there," he whispered, "We'll get you sorted."

The earthworm coiled its way around the boy's outstretched finger, and immediately the boy moved his other hand under the first to cup his precious cargo. He slowly stood, then looked around for a dry spot of land.

A pot of petunias was thrust under his nose by the stallholder next to him. "Small deeds may seem small at first, but so do seeds," a gravelly voice said. "Some stay small, others become the foundations for greatness. Your friend can rest here until there is a drier home for him."

The boy smiled up at the man in the wide brimmed leather hat and cloak, and gratefully deposited his charge in the much drier soil of the pot. Within seconds, the worm had tunnelled its way down and disappeared.

The man's stall was covered in a dazzling array of goods, everything from small trinkets on leather thonging, to a massive statue of some form of cat the like of which he had never seen before and must have taken at least three men to lift. Strange, dried herbs and flowers lined one edge of the multi-hued tent, hung upside down from a string that ran the length of the wall. A rack of warm-looking cloaks sat towards the front, and a glass fronted cabinet filled with coloured bottles glinted in the back. The man was standing behind a table on which lay knives, pieces of knotted cord, small bundles of twigs, a box filled with live frogs, and (of course) a potted pink petunia plant.

The man himself was nothing much to look at. His ample frame was mostly hidden beneath an oiled leather cloak, which, in conjunction with the hat, made him look rather non-descript and brown. The round face was red and pockmarked, and topped with faded, ginger hair (which also seemed to infest his square beard and moustache in the places it wasn't white). He propped himself up with a walking stick which seemed to have a lot more "stick" quality than it had "walk" quality. In fact, if it weren't for the strangeness of the wares, the boy would have thought this man a simple farmer.

Just as he was thinking that he should ask the man about how he had managed to transport the stone cat, he was thumped on the back by a hard fist.

"What's with the geez', runt?" shouted Reginald.

Reginald was always bad news, especially when he was in a group. Many of the local boys had decided it was better to join forces with the butcher's son rather than risk falling foul of his frequent attacks, and so were often seen in his company. This only seemed to feed his desire to cause trouble. Today, he had three in tow. The boy steeled himself; a pack this size could only mean he was today's chosen target.

"What geese? I think you're turning a bit blind there, Reginald," the boy said, choosing to risk all to save himself from looking weak. Weakness was bad; it only encouraged Reginald to pick more often.

Reginald looked slightly confused for a second, then his face cleared and he actually laughed. "Not geese, idiot, geez'. As in geezer! This old fart!"

The boy took a deep breath through his nose. "Nope," he said with a confidence he didn't feel inside, "That's not the smell of fart, all I smell is rain."

The boys in Reginald's party were starting to titter softly, as Reginald's face clouded in confusion again. Then a slight chuckle escaped the lips of the onlooking marketeer, and all confusion was gone. The butcher's boy changed his focus to the adult, a sneer on his face.

"You, old fart. I mean you. I know everyone in town, and you're not from here. That means you're from SOMEWHERE ELSE!" He said this as if it were a revelation to the world. "That means you're not from here. My da says people like you are no good. My da says people like you are Not Worth A Pinch. My da says people like you are better off far away and never setting foot in town, and if it were up to him he'd hunt the lot of you!"

"Your da says a lot of things about people he's never met and never will, doesn't he?" the man replied calmly, "Nevertheless, I'm not from somewhere else, I live barely an hour's ride from here, and I know a good deal more about the goings on in this town than Reginald Cutler, the butcher's son, is likely to," (Reginald blanched a little at being identified so easily), "and it's high time you filled your head with a lot more than 'My da said...'"

The bully looked at his group uneasily, then turned his attention to the stock-laden table. "What are you, some sort of weirdo who runs around the forest eating berries and living in trees? You're trying to sell useless bits of rope and bundles of twigs! If I wanted twigs, I could pick them up off the ground myself!" He grabbed one of the offending bundles from the table.

"I wouldn't untie that if I were you," warned the amused-looking man with a grin on his face.

In response, Reginald looked directly into the man's eyes and pulled on the red ribbon holding the sticks together. It fell away from the bundle, and for a count of two there was triumph in his eyes, then suddenly...

WHOOSH!...

The bundle exploded into fire in Reginald's hands.

Reginald hurled them from his grasp in surprise, and, for a moment, all was silent except for the slight hiss as each stick fell to the ground and doused itself in the wetness. Then it was his turn to explode.

"What do you mean by that? Trying to set me on fire, you could've gotten me killed, you moron! I'll tell my da on you!"

"That's quite all right, please do, as either you or he will be paying for that merchandise. Two crowns for a bundle of sixty fire starters. I'm sure your father will be most pleased to be so far out of pocket..."

Reginald flushed red, turned, and ran, his cronies laughing at his fleeing back. They were, after all, here for the show and nothing more.

"... and I'll catch up with him whether you tell him or not," finished the man quietly. "Now," he turned his attention back to the other boys, "What can I do for you all?"

But all the boys acted as if they couldn't see the tent, or even recall that it was here. They wandered over to the fishing rods they'd piled against the wall of a nearby house, chatting about how poorly their fishing had gone that morning.

All bar one, the first, the boy with the worm, who was studying the other bundles of sticks closely.

The man smiled. "So, young man, is there anything I can do for you?" he repeated.

The boy looked up with an intense expression on his face. "How do they work?" he demanded.

"Oh, that's quite simple, you pull one from the bundle and it lights. No real difficulty in it, you just need to make certain the ribbon remains."

"No," grumbled the boy, "How do they work? How do they light?"

"Even simpler, it's magic."

The boy seemed to be becoming quite agitated now. "No, how do they work? There's got to be some method that makes them like they are, they don't just fall off a tree like that. Why do adults always do this; they tell you it's magic but they don't tell you how! Don't you know?"

"Of course I know," said the man. "I'm a wizard. I made them."

He thought for a second, then continued, "The magic is not in the sticks. The magic is in the ribbon. A lot of things have potential to be something bigger than they are. Sticks have potential to burn. The ribbon is a catalyst to release that potential. But you limit what it does by tying a knot in it, because knots are powerful binding magic. When your pudgy friend untied that knot, it released *all* the energy, rather than just a little."

The boy thought about that for a little bit. "Why did all the boys go away?" he asked. "They knew you were here, then they just sort of forgot. It was weird."

"Oh, it happens," said the wizard nonchalantly.

"Occasionally something will break the geas on the tent, and children get through. Not often though. You were invited in, which, I suppose, is why you can still see me, but most don't ever see my tent until their majority, when they have the money to pay for what they break. I'm not quite certain of the details of the particular spell; it's not one of mine, see?" he explained. "Back in my youth, I got if off a sorcerer who had a rather nasty run-in with a salamander shortly afterward. He never did tell me the trick. I was just a hedge-mage back then, I lacked the deeper understanding I have now."

"What's the difference," asked the boy, "between a wizard and all that other stuff?"

The wizard took a deep breath and frowned. "I suppose you're going to keep asking me all manner of questions, aren't you?"

The boy nodded.

"Well then, you'd better sit down, there's a lot to answer and that doesn't happen quickly."

The wizard gestured to a pair of chairs that the boy hadn't noticed earlier. The boy sat, and for the next few hours the wizard explained about the different types of magic and the way different people used it. Every now and then, someone would stop to buy something, and the wizard would rise to speak to them, addressing each by his or her name and asking them about their children, their pets, their jobs. The boy marvelled each time that someone so familiar with the town and its residents could be completely unknown to him, who had spent his entire ten years of existence within the confines of its limited number of streets. The people who visited the stall didn't seem to see the boy, however, much in the same way as the boys before had lost the ability to see the stall or its inhabitant.

Not, that is, until late in the afternoon, when his mother came flouncing by.

"Good afternoon, Felicity," the man called out politely. The boy's mother turned with an expression the boy had never seen on his mother's face before.

"Normie, darling," she cried, "Oh, it's been simply ages! I missed you!"

Then she spotted the boy in the background, and her face took on a look of thunder. "You! You little brat, where have you been hiding? I've been looking for you everywhere!" She turned again to the wizard. "What's he been up to, he hasn't nicked anything has he?"

"No, Felicity," he said, "He and I have just been having a little chat..."

She turned once again to the boy. "You've been bugging him, haven't you? You and your infernal questions, how many times have I told you..."

The man cut her off with a hasty "...No, wait, it's okay. He's been quite good. He's a credit to you."

At this, the boy's mother stopped fuming at the boy and turned her attention back to the man with a beam on her face.

"Well, that's not so bad then, is it?" she said, almost to herself.

The wizard continued, "I actually wanted to speak to you about your son. He's quite bright, and I think he'd do well in my employ."

For once, Felicity seemed at a loss for words. She stared at the man, her mouth half open, small sounds of half formed words popping from her in small gasps.

"I would, of course, reimburse the both of you for your troubles. I know that since the death of your husband the boy has been of great assistance to you, but I'm sure that twenty crowns a month would be sufficient."

"Tuh-twenty?" she gasped out. Twenty crowns was a fortune, and her head started filling with dreams of avarice.

"Five for your troubles, and fifteen as wages for the boy, to be set aside by you for his majority. I will clothe and feed him, which will lessen the financial burden upon your shoulders. He will, of course, live with me, as my tower is too far away for idle wandering to and from; however, you will be welcome to visit as often as you find convenient. Terms of employment will be renegotiated once the boy reaches his majority in eight years."

The boy thought. Five crowns a month was ten times what his mother was making with her small embroidery store, and more than enough to keep her comfortable. "I think it's a good deal, mum," he said.

She was already nodding in agreement, barely noting her child's assent. She had married, and given birth, young, and her husband had died while she was still pregnant. The ten years since had been years of stolen youth, shackled, she had thought at times, by the child she had borne. She was not yet thirty and longed for the freedom to act like a girl again. "The boy's yours," she blurted out. "Twenty crowns a month."

"Well, I see we're all in agreement," said the wizard with a smile on his face. He pulled a strange coin from his pocket. "This is a wizard contract," he stated, putting the coin to his lips and repeating the terms he had already given. He placed it on the table. "We each place a finger on the coin to give our assent to the terms."

The boy immediately placed his finger on the coin.

The wizard looked at Felicity, who seemed hesitant. Tales abounded of wizard contracts forfeited. The tales were never pretty. Then the thought of the money rallied her, and she touched the coin gingerly, as if it were something slimy and unpleasant.

The wizard placed his finger last upon the coin.

Nothing momentous happened, and Felicity let out a loud breath and relaxed. Her hand fell away from the coin.

"So, what happens now?" asked the child, not certain what to do with his finger now it was on the coin.

The wizard winked and picked up the coin from the table. "Hold out your hand, boy," he commanded.

The boy did as he was told, and the wizard clasped his arm

forearm firmly. "Don't worry, this won't hurt a bit," he said softly, and pressed the coin to the boy's wrist.

Light flared from the coin, and the boy gasped in surprise as the golden disc sank painlessly into his skin. After about a minute, it had become entirely covered with skin, and a red-brown tattoo formed, replicating the coin that lay underneath.

The wizard looked at Felicity. "Your son's flesh will be marked by our agreement until his eighteenth birthday, at which time the agreement is negated. If anyone fails to uphold their end of the bargain, they pay in flesh also. It's different from contract to contract—the magic decides which way it will flow, but it's generally not pleasant. Let's all steer clear of that, shall we?"

Then he turned to the boy. "Well, Peter, it's getting on. Let's get packing, it's time to go home..."

Chapter 2

---

661 OM Tarandeer
Year of the Tangled Briar

Norman's Tower

The cat watched from the rafters as Peter entered the room, arm lifted to shield his face from the heat. He took a few steps, then stopped at the edge of the chalk circle, staring at the plume of flame that issued from the pedestal in the centre of the room (and, coincidentally, the centre of the chalk circle). He carefully made his way around the edge of the room, watching the flame as if it were a snake about to strike. As he moved, he frequently stopped to check various things he passed: under the bed, behind the bookshelf, inside the cupboard. Eventually Peter had circumnavigated the room, still looking warily at the fire and unwilling to step across the line of chalk.

"Norman, are you there?" issued tentatively from his lips.

The cat could have told Peter where Norman was, but Peter hadn't asked her. Peter barely seemed to notice her these days, so two could play at that game.

She wondered why Peter didn't use his magic to find Norman. She could smell it in him, a great, throbbing pool of force, trapped away where nobody could get to it except Peter.

But then again, he never used it, much to everybody's bewilderment and frustration.

He was circling the room again, looking everywhere he had looked before, and some places he hadn't, like behind the mirror and under Norman's pile of dirty socks, calling "Norman?" softly each time he lifted an object or opened a drawer.

Of course, Norman wasn't answering. Norman wasn't here. But she wasn't going to tell him that. Not until he spoke to her first, she decided.

Eventually Peter gave up looking for his master, and left the room with many worried, backward glances.

The cat gave the book between her paws a last lick, rose from her beam and climbed quietly down from her perch, using the bookshelf, the cupboard, and the bed as staging areas. Finally, she came to a halt at the edge of the chalk circle. Sniffing the line that had worried Peter so greatly, she could detect nothing of concern, so she stepped over it and walked up to the pedestal.

This was more interesting. Now that she stood here, she could see the small gold ring from which the flame was issuing.

To the cat's sensitive nose, it smelt like warm cinnamon rolls straight from the oven, and she started to lap at the fire, drinking the magic that was issuing steadily from the ring.

Chapter 3

APPRENTICE

653 OM Tarandeer
Year of the Leaping Rabbit

Pugton

The boy looked to the wizard for instructions. Felicity had wandered off, wearing the same vacant expression that had graced the faces of the boys earlier.

"I can help pack up, and I'll be careful," he ventured, "but I don't think I'll be able to help you move your cat." He looked at the statue pointedly. "How did you get it here in the first place?"

The wizard let out a loud, rolling belly-laugh. "Oh, we don't need to worry about Suzie here," he grinned, "She can take care of herself!"

Norman tickled the statue under the chin, and to Peter's surprise the cat looked at him and started purring.

"She's a gargoyle," Norman explained. "Artists have a power all of their own, and sometimes, very rarely, they infuse their own life into that of their artwork. A while back it was happening quite a lot because a lot of the priesthood were doing those odd-looking sculptures for churches, and the naming convention stuck, but don't let that change the way you look at our Suzie here, she's a sweetheart."

"Wow. What does she eat?"

"Magic. She doesn't need a lot, just enough to keep the life force from being burnt out on her movement. After all, energy is energy, and it all has to come from somewhere. She eats my failures and the tailings from spent magic." He held out the ribbon that Reginald had dropped earlier, and the cat gently took it in her mouth and swallowed it down. "Waste not, want not, I always say."

Peter stared at the cat in fascination and a stream of questions fell from his lips, "May I pat her? Will she bite me? What sort of cat is she? She's so big. Who made her?"

"Yes, you may pat her, no, she won't bite you, except of course if you're threatening her or people she cares about. As for the type of cat, she's a leopard, but there's some artistic licence been taken, so she looks somewhat different from leopards in the wild. I have no idea who the artist was, but they did a masterful job.

"She just wandered into the tower one day. Gargoyles do tend to be drawn to wizards; quite often if they don't find one soon enough, they starve to death. It's a trade-off; I help her, and she helps me.

"And just so you know, Suzie is quite intelligent. Don't go treating her like a cat or a dog; she has as much intelligence as you or I. She reads quite voraciously. Her mouth is the wrong shape to speak in the human fashion, but if need be, she can scratch down words on slate."

The cat nodded in response to the wizard's comments, then looked expectantly at Peter. He reached out a hand to her neck. It was cold and hard, with the grainy texture of sandstone, and he was jolted into the realisation that she was made of rock.

"Wow, you're awesome!" he said to Suzie. The he turned to Norman, who had opened a large satchel and was placing the chairs into it. "How does she help you?" he asked.

The chairs seemed to become engulfed by the bag and disappear.

"Well, in this instance she helps me with carting my wares to and from town, and sometimes she's able to help with setup and pack down. Much more of a help than you seem to be at the moment," he pointed out, and Peter looked embarrassed. He turned to the table covered in knick-knacks.

"What do you want me to pack, where do you want me to pack it, and how do I do it without turning myself into a hedgehog?" he asked.

It turns out there was nothing much for him to do after all. The live frogs would not allow Peter anywhere near them, setting off piercing sirens whenever he approached. This, it seems, was their purpose in life; Norman had dubbed them "alarm frogs" and sold them to nobles who worried about theft or poachers. Peter was forced to back up quite a distance while Norman quieted them and then placed them into his hat, which then went firmly back onto his head.

The boy, standing in the middle of what had previously been a bustling road filled with buyers, watched the smooth operation of wizard and statue-cat as they worked in fluid concert with each other. He felt that he was a point of discord, that there was no point in their dance that he would be able to fit in. He looked down, afraid that he might have made a mistake.

There, in the mud between his feet, he spotted a curve. It wasn't anything of note, just a line on the ground, but it didn't seem natural.

He bent down to wipe away the mud, and a gleam of silver was his reward. Quickly, he grabbed the coin, and it came away from the ground with a slight sucking sound. His worries momentarily forgotten, Peter rushed to show his new friends his unexpected treasure.

"Well done!" was the response from Norman, who then thrust the petunia pot into Peter's hands. "Hold onto this, will you?"

The cat simply responded with a single raised eyebrow. She

was uninterested in anything that wasn't magical, and coins didn't count.

The pieces of rope, twigs, and knives were deemed too dangerous for a ten-year old boy, so were dealt with by Norman, who simply tied them all up in the tablecloth they rested on with no fuss or bother. There was no table beneath the cloth to pack, and the boy was left marvelling at the fabric that had seemed so solid only moments ago.

The cloak rack, including all the cloaks on it, folded down into a small cube, which got thrown haphazardly into the satchel. The rattling cabinet at the back took similar treatment, except it was placed carefully into a pocket on the side of the bag.

Finally, the tent, hanging goods included, was folded up by Norman and Suzie working in unison, and miraculously altered to form a cart, already harnessed to the big, stone cat.

"Wonderful job!" beamed Norman. "You played a pivotal role; we couldn't have done it as quickly without you. Now hop on board, and we'll be off!"

Peter was still holding the petunia pot in his hands and couldn't quite work out how to climb into the cart without putting it down first. Finally, he was forced to hand it back to Norman in order to climb up.

"I wonder how your friend is doing in here, Peter?" he asked, then looked closely into the foliage of the flowering bush. After a moment, he stepped up onto the cart, his longer legs meaning he didn't require both hands to ascend.

"Keep an eye on her, she'll be one to watch for," he commented, as he handed the pot back to the boy, who was now comfortably seated. Then, with hardly a jolt, Suzie set off at a lope.

Peter, confused by the comment, parted the leaves in search of an explanation. What he saw was the oddest thing he had ever seen (even including everything he had experienced today). The worm he had rescued was twined around the stem of the petunia plant. The worm seemed to be looking directly at him, and sparks suddenly emitted from that end.

Norman reached into a pocket and drew out a magnifying glass, which he passed to Peter.

"Take a good look; that's no ordinary worm you saved today," he said, and the boy took the glass.

Peering into a world of magnification, he was shocked to see legs and wings on his 'worm'. Without the aid of the glass, if he squinted, he could just make out the faintest traces of the extra appendages, but he would never have thought to look otherwise.

"What you've stumbled across today, my boy," intoned the bearded man by his side, "is not a worm, but a wyrm. A female one at that. She'll grow to be a dragon, if she survives this stage of her life. Most don't, but you've just got her through one hurdle. She probably would have drowned, or died of exhaustion, or been eaten by a bird, if you hadn't rescued her this morning."

"Really? A dragon?" Peter was excited. "What colour will she be? How do you know she's a girl? Does she collect treasure? What's her name? Is she..."

"Woah! Slow down! I need to be able to remember your questions to answer them!

"She looks to be a red, which is why I didn't notice what she was straight off the bat. It's easy to miss the red dragons, as they do tend to be the same colour as earthworms early in life.

"I know she's a girl because she's sparking. Only female dragons breathe fire; not many people know that. I think it's so they can defend their young better. They tend to be very protective of their young. How this dragon came to be here, I have no idea, I haven't heard of any dragon lairs nearby, and it's odd to see one without its mother nearby.

"She will collect treasure, but at the moment she's very small, so she won't have any yet.

"And what else did you ask? Oh, yes, her name. She'll get to choose that when she's a bit bigger."

Peter thought about that for a moment. Then he pulled his

newly found silver coin from his pocket. "Dragons need treasure, don't they?" he asked.

Norman looked at the boy through narrowed eyes. "Yes," he said slowly, "they need to eat metals to grow healthily. They don't eat much, but they hoard it for times when it's not so easy to find. What do you have in mind?"

"I don't need this money, but she does. So, I'm giving her this silver so she grows big and strong!" With that, Peter thrust the coin's edge into the soil of the pot, burying it halfway. Hurriedly, the tiny wyrm uncoiled from the plant, and made its way to the coin. She wrapped herself tightly around it and seemed to be kissing it.

Looking through the glass, Peter could see the truth of it. Not having a mouth large enough to bite into the metal, she was licking it with a long tongue.

"I'm not sure that was the wisest thing to do," stated the wizard firmly. "Dragons are not pets and shouldn't be treated as such. I don't mind if you help her out, but it could lead to trouble later."

"I don't think helping someone get food is ever a bad thing to do," Peter stated flatly. "If I were her, I'd think it was good that someone helped me, and I would then want to help other people in the same way."

Norman grinned. "Good! I like it that you own your decision. Just remember that she has to do things on her own. She's intelligent, just like you, or I, or Suzie, and she needs the ability to make her own way in the world."

They continued on their bumpy way home. They had left the road and were now making their way through an overgrown field, with not even the trace of a goat track to mark their way.

Peter's forehead furrowed. "Does Suzie know where she's going?" he asked Norman with concern.

"Oh yes," Norman answered nonchalantly, "It's always the scenic route to the tower. Can't be going the same way twice." He winked at Peter. "You can't get unwanted visitors if nobody knows the way, can you?"

"But how is Mum going to find me, if nobody knows the way? You said she could visit."

A chuckle came from beneath the beard. "I don't think that's going to be a problem. When your mother is determined to do something, do it she will. Determination is a magic unto itself and can bend time and space if it's correctly applied. She'll find us, just wait and see."

So, Peter sat and watched the world move past the cart, one bumpy tussock of grass at a time. From time to time, he peered in at the small passenger in the pot plant in his lap. She seemed to be sleeping, still wrapped tightly around the coin.

Soon, a small tower appeared, and his stomach started to clench as the realisation suddenly set in...

This was his new life now.

Chapter 4

THE BLAZE

661 OM Tarandeer
Year of the Tangled Briar

Norman's Tower

A thin beam of sunlight lanced through the bushes and fell across the eye of the sleeping dragon.

Petunia cracked the eye open and considered whether or not the day deserved her attention. A thin veneer of snow covered the ground beyond her bush, and she considered how cold it might be outside of her pocket of warmth. But she could see the puffs of smoke arising from the tower chimney, and logic would suggest that inside would be warmer than out.

She turned to her daily hoard count while she mulled over the options.

Petunia's hoard was an odd assortment of broken jewellery, random lengths of chain, and small coins that Peter picked up occasionally when he went into town. Slowly she licked each one, eyes closed and half asleep, savouring the varied metallic tastes. The copper penny, found and offered to her just days ago; the length of rusted iron chain she had found herself a month past; the thin, gold-plated piece of twisted metal that may once have been a ring, slipped from a finger while swimming; the zinc wire which had been grudgingly given up by the wizard himself after much cajoling; the handle from a brass vase...

Each item was revered by the tiny dragon, taking her time with each as lovingly as the one before. One by one they were catalogued, with Petunia saving the best for last.

The silver coin was the most precious item amongst the hoard she had so painstakingly arranged. She had determined long ago that this was the one item she would never eat, no matter how desperate she became. This was the foundation of her hoard, and even if she lost everything else, this one piece would bolster her to start again. It was the first.

Lazily she reached a long tongue out to touch her prize. The air was cool on the moist parts of her mouth, and she extended her neck further, groping for it.

Her tongue met only dirt.

With surprise, she opened her eyes, which affirmed what her tongue her already told her. The silver coin was gone! She huffed in alarm, and a faint puff of flame burst from her mouth, accidentally setting fire to her bush.

Hurriedly, she backed out of her cozy hole, small keening sounds issuing from the back of her throat as she watched her home steadily catch more alight, and the silver coin still was gone.

Thieves! she thought. She had heard stories from Peter's lips about people fighting, killing, sneaking into dragon's lairs, all to take their treasures. In these stories the dragons never won, because they were all written by men. But she remembered older stories, from her mother, of fighting and winning, of punishing those who sought to steal.

This is the worst thing that has ever happened to me, she thought, as she tried to snatch her remaining hoard pieces from the fire. Then she amended that statement in her head. This was *almost* the worst thing that had ever happened to her.

She thought back to that day, the day Peter had found her squirming in the mud. The worst thing had happened on that day.

Suddenly she knew. The boy! The mean boy! He must have taken it! Her child-like mind latched onto the only person she had ever met who had ever been unkind to her.

Giving up on her hoard pieces (the blaze was quite ferocious at this point) she rose into the air and sped as fast as she could to the tower.

"Worms!" the dark-haired child cried, "Look, there's worms all over the place!"

"They'll make good bait," said the skinny one, "We could grab a heap and go fishing."

"Nah, fishing's boring," said the pimply one.

"Dare you to eat one," the fat boy said.

"Who, me?" asked the boy with dark hair in alarm. "Yuck, no way!"

The fat boy had not been looking at anyone in particular when he had made his dare, but he seized onto this opportunity.

"What are you, chicken?" he jeered, setting the other two off into cries of "Chi-ken, chi-ken, chi-ken..."

"You can't say no to a dare, that's not an option. You have to eat one."

"No," the boy cried. "I don't want to!"

"You're going to eat a worm," the fat boy said firmly. Then he tackled the smaller boy, dropping him to the floor. Laughingly, the other two held down the boy's arms as the fat boy sat astride him, attempting to force his jaws open. Failing in this, he then resorted to peeling back the boy's lips and mashing the worm against the boy's teeth, tucking the remnants into his cheeks. Having at least partially succeeded, he hopped off the boy, and the other two released him, still laughing.

"What's it taste like, Brian?" the skinny boy giggled.

Brian was busy spitting out chunks of the red-brown creature from his mouth, grimacing in disgust. He turned a sarcastic glance the skinny boy's way. "Try one and find out," he suggested, "They're delicious."

Then he went back to spitting and scrubbing his mouth out with his fingers.

"Hey, have you ever tried cutting a worm in half?" asked the fat one, with a nasty leer. "They just grow back, leave 'em for a while and they do, they grow back."

"Betcha they don't," said the boy with pimples. "I reckon they just die."

The fat one pulled out a pocketknife. "Here, I'll show you!"

Then with a flick of the wrist, one worm was in two halves. Two very dead halves.

The fat boy stared at it, confused. "Must've been on its way already," he finally decided, and tried another. And another. And another.

Each died as quickly as the one before, and soon he had a pile of a dozen dead worms.

Eventually he tired of his experiment. "Must be a different kind of worm," he shrugged. "Fish bait it is then, boys. Grab yourselves a pocketful."

With that, the boys all grabbed handfuls of the wriggling creatures, stuffing them in their pockets, until they had picked up every last one.

The skinny one straightened from his task, looking at the emaciated, horse-sized dragon beside him, who was making odd noises from the back of its throat and struggling to free itself. He stepped further away from its head, which was shackled tightly to the ground in front of a large furnace.

"So, Reggie, where'd your dad get it?"

The fat one kicked a declawed, iron-bound, back leg. "Some trader over in Nock. Gave him some bull story about how he could heat his house for free and sell the wyrmlings, so Da paid a bunch. Well, it laid an egg, and it was here for ages, but the baby either died or escaped since last time I was here a couple weeks ago, because it's gone and there ain't been no little dragon. Plus it's useless, you gotta keep it chained up all over so it can't move an inch, because it bites all the shackles if it can get to 'em. It eats a beast a week, but it won't just eat the meat, you've got to shove it right in its mouth or it won't feed itself. Da says it's costing him more than it was worth. Says he got ripped, eh?"

"Don't they talk or something?" asked Brian, who had finished cleaning out his mouth and now was acting as if nothing had occurred.

"It cussed Da out good and well!" Reggie replied. "Da didn't like that, so its tongue came out, just yesterday."

Then they left the basement, shutting the door on the tears pouring from the dragon's eyes, heading out through the market with their fishing rods.

Jostling and punching each other as they made their way through the stalls toward the river, none of them noticed as a single worm fell from Reginald's pocket.

Petunia's eyes welled up as she thought of that day when she had lost every one of her family. Ripped from a mother who had been chained into slavery, forced to watch the slaughter of her siblings, Peter and Norman were all she had.

Most young dragons would spend the first decade in their mother's care, passing through their most dangerous years under her close tutelage until they were large enough to be able to fight off most predators. Even so, those first years were still fraught with danger, and out of the 70-80 wyrmlings in any hatching, roughly two thirds would die. But having all die on the same day was unheard of, and the grief remained inside her like a throbbing wound.

Through blurry vision, she made her way into the tower via the unglazed window slit that housed Peter's water-carrier.

"Where are you?" she shouted, winging about the room at an unsafe speed. "I need you! Where are you? Come here now!"

She was still shouting when Peter came stumbling up the stairs, bleary eyed from his broken sleep. He had lain awake for hours, ears straining for a hint of a footstep or creak of a floorboard, but the tower had screamed its silent emptiness to him, each second beating upon his chest like a tabor.

"What is it?" he yawned. "Can't it wait?"

"NO! IT CAN'T WAIT!" yelled Petunia, "WHERE'S NORMAN WE NEED TO GO WE NEED TO GO NOW WE NEED TO GET IT BACK WE NEED TO GET THE BOY HE TOOK IT IT MUST BE HIM..."

As she shouted, louder and louder, she sped faster and faster around the bewildered teen until finally she flew with a

THUNK!

straight into a ceiling beam. Her tiny body crumpled to the floor, and with concern, Peter rushed to cradle her tiny form in his hands. At eight years old, she was still no larger than his palm (excluding her incredibly lengthy tail, which drooped down past his elbow). Norman's explanation had always been that dragons grow incredibly slowly, but that they never stopped growing, so the house sized creatures from stories were thousands of years old.

She looked so fragile in his hands, and Peter felt suddenly overwhelmed by the events of the night. Where had Norman disappeared to? He'd never left Peter alone in the tower before, and he had no idea what to do, or if Norman was alright, or how to even light the fire without the handy firestarters that Norman kept upstairs.

Fire, he thought. A fire would be handy right about now. A faint waft of woodsmoke tingled in his nostrils as a reminder.

Fire! he thought. He hadn't lit it yet, so why was the smell so pervasive? He rushed to the window, and there he saw it, the blazing bush, tongues of flame licking high in search of more fuel, threatening branches from a neighbouring tree.

Peter looked around wildly, searching for a safe spot to deposit his charge. But this floor was desolate of soft or warm. Giving up on anywhere to put her, he tucked her petite form into his hip pocket, curling her tail up and tucking it in beside her so that it wouldn't tangle with his legs. Then, grabbing the wash-bucket from its hook by the window, he leaped for the stairs, bounding down them two at a time, and out the front door.

Bypassing the well entirely, Peter ran for the tiny trickle of a stream that passed by the tower. Barely enough to get your ankles wet, he and Norman used to joke, and it was true. He scooped at the water with the bucket, but there was not enough depth to submerge it fully, and with each scoop, less than a quarter of the bucket was filled. But scoop he did, and with each scoop, he threw what little water he had gleaned over the blazing fire. One scoop, two, three, four, five... and with each, a tiny hiss of steam from where it had landed. Turning to look, Peter saw that the blaze reclaimed its lost territory almost as quickly as the water had doused it.

"Aaaarrrgh!" he cried at the fire, every iota of his will draining into that one sound, throwing the water, bucket and all, towards the bush. And with that sound, a release, like a cork popping, and an impossible amount of water fountained out of the bucket, as Peter collapsed onto the stony shore. Then the tears came. Angry, frustrated, howling, exhausting, burning wet furrows letting out the pain of being alone and scared and overwhelmed.

Chapter 5

661 OM Tarandeer
Year of the Tangled Briar

Norman's Tower

Norman's sleep had been rudely interrupted by an all too familiar voice directly in his ear.

"You're needed, boy!" it shouted at him, causing him to violently jerk awake, falling off the bed and onto the raw wooden floor of his third-floor laboratory space.

A slow sizzle filled the room, hot and hissing, and a yellow glow emanated from the pedestal routinely used for isolating volatile items he was handling at any particular time. Grabbing a stick of chalk, he drew a quick retardant perimeter to halt the spread of any spontaneous floor combustion, then he stepped forward, one steady step at a time, trying to ignore the sweat that had newly formed on his forehead and was now trickling into his eyes.

Within the glow was a small, yellow flame, and within that flame he witnessed a thing he had never dared imagine... a golden ring was building itself in the heart of the flame.

He considered it closely — fast teleport he was familiar with, but this seemed to be a slow teleport, potentially atoms at a time.

The heat, he surmised, was probably a result of friction as atoms were suddenly shifted to make way for the new matter.

Norman took a deep breath in, filling his lungs, then let it slowly, taking a moment to think. Then he quietly pulled some emergency items together, floating them silently towards him from areas around the tower.

"Suzie," he said to the gargoyle he knew was sitting in the rafters, "Sorry to put this on you, but I need to head out rather suddenly. Could you please look after Peter while I'm gone? Who knows what he'll get up to without me. If he asks, tell him I'm taking care of something important, and I'll make sure I'm back before his birthday. And it's okay to have a lick, but don't eat the entire teleport when I leave; I want to study it later to see how it works. I'll get you something nice instead when I get back. Thank you."

Bracing himself for the potential of mutilation or horrendous agony, he poked a calloused finger at the tiny piece of gold…

…And was suddenly somewhere else.

His muscles clenched as bare feet reacted to the transition from warm wood to cold stone, and he started to shiver. This place was far darker than the room he had been in, and spots formed in front of his eyes as he strained to see. But slowly, he started to make put a pile of clothing lying only a few paces away, and then suddenly he could see that this pile wasn't simply clothing — there was a person lying crumpled on the floor.

"Albert!" Norman rushed to the side of the collapsed man. The steady rise and fall of Albert's chest reassured him that his mentor and friend still lived, although at this distance he could hear that the man's breathing rattled and wheezed.

With gentleness, he snuck his arms under Albert's shoulders and knees, lifting him from the cold floor. The realisation that his once teacher was now so light and frail was shocking to him, and he did his best to not jostle the elderly mage as he carried him to the small cot set against the wall.

Things in Albert's hall were much as they had been decades ago when Norman had spent his younger years here. He remembered this space, sunk into the side of a mountain, the walls smoothed as if someone had melted them into glass. Pots of glisterweed along the walls or on the frequent shelving that jutted directly from the stone lit the space with a soft, orange light. Each room was neat and ordered, with none of the clutter that Norman preferred to surround himself with.

He put the same old kettle onto the familiar hob, then reached for the white-glazed pottery cannister for the tea that sat in its habitual spot. How had it survived all this time, he wondered, as it must have already been old when he was just a boy? Nostalgia burned hot, unshed tears in the corners of his eyes as he worried about the mage in the next room.

Norman looked down at himself, realising that he was here only in a night-frock. That would make things difficult, he considered, as his bladder started to press upon his needs. The thing with digging a home into the side of a mountain is that some mountains are in inconvenient places. Albert's mountain was in a very inconvenient place, and the coolness of this room was nothing compared to the icy wasteland he would have to traverse to reach the outhouse (which was, inconveniently, outside).

He sighed and moved towards the annexe—a group of rooms Albert had dug specifically for Norman's apprenticeship and which he assumed had been repurposed for additional storage or other apprentices. Passing through the doorway, he moved automatically across to his wardrobe and pulled out an old, favoured cloak. And he halted.

Scanning across the room, a pair of shoes was nestled beneath the bed. A scatter of things—odd socks, random bits of paper, a broken-nibbed quill—lay strewn on the rumpled bedspread. A few old journals slumped sideways on shelving. The desk by the bed housed a wide but shallow wooden box with a lattice framework inside, each section painstakingly inked with a description of the powders that had once filled it.

Norman ran his fingers over the smooth wood. Barring a thin layer of dust, it was just as he had left it on his eighteenth birthday.

The shoes would be handy, he thought. And socks, no matter how odd. Then, with a sudden spurt of memory, he fell to his knees and reached under the bed. Yes! It was still here, the open crate that had been the final resting place for his outdoor clothing. Swiftly he pulled on his full fleece — pants, coat, hat, and finally the wool-lined boots — and braved the path to the snowy outdoors.

By the time he returned, the kettle had just started to whistle, and he gratefully poured the steaming liquid into the two cups with dried leaves in the bottom. A little honey into both, and he carefully carried them back into the workshop where he had left Albert. He pulled a chair and a small table over to the small cot, which had never been intended as a permanent bed. It was here for those days when the work was too taxing and the walk back to the bedroom was too far.

"Boy," the elderly man croaked, "What took you so long? I've been waiting…"

Norman sighed with relief, a smile flitting across his face at his mentor's consciousness.

"I got here as quickly as I could. I have tea, if you're able?"

Norman propped Albert up to sip at the sweet tea. Feeling the sharp bones of Albert's spine pressing into his shoulder, he shifted, placing the bulk of his body behind the man's back to give him some stability.

"I'll get you into your bedroom once you feel strong enough to walk. You seemed to be in quite a state when I arrived."

Albert heaved a breath, followed by a rattling cough that shook his frail body. Panting from the exertion, he squeezed out, "Just a moment or two and I'll be right, but a hand would not go amiss."

Chapter 6

Fear

653 OM Tarandeer
Year of the Leaping Rabbit

Pugton

Felicity shivered, rubbing her arms vigorously against the chill of the night air.

Peter had been gone two weeks and she was reaching the end of her stored supply of chopped wood. The axe against the wall was his tool; she'd not held onto it in years. The boy had always seemed to enjoy the wanton destruction of the logs he would drag from the brush, and she allowed him his small joys. Unfortunately, there was not enough time in the day for searching the brush for timber and her meagre income was too scarce to buy it.

She placed a few more precious twigs onto the fire, seeking to eke out the last scraps of warmth.

The small house was silent without Peter, empty sounding, empty feeling, like a void was waiting to be filled. At first, it had seemed as if it would be a good thing, and Felicity had pottered around the small house in a frenzy of cleaning, tidying up after the child who wouldn't be staying there for the near future, packing away unneeded items and stripping the small bed of its linens. But, as the hours wore on, the silence seemed to press upon her ears more and more.

Just as she had every night this week, Felicity had cooked too much, and having eaten her usual fill, she looked at the extra portion. *Better eaten than wasted,* she thought, considering the likelihood that it would spoil over the evening, and tucked in, forcing herself to eat every bite, sopping up the gravy with the heel of bread, until she felt like she might burst.

Felicity looked around aimlessly for something to occupy her but there was nothing to do. The room was neat, neater than it had been for a decade. With a sigh she prepared herself for bed, knowing that she would just toss and turn but seeking a refuge from the emptiness, the void of Peter.

The small movements consumed her utterly until suddenly she stopped. Was that a noise outside, beneath the eave? She pulled her shawl closer around her shoulders. Quietly, she crept to the door, listening hard.

"It's nothing," she said quietly, using her own voice to show her that she hadn't become totally deaf.

The soft thump repeated itself.

"It's kids. Bloody kids," she swore, heaving herself out of the bed with discomfort.

As she reached for her dressing gown, once more she heard a soft thump against the door. The soft sound of footsteps padding outside screamed into her keenly focussed ears, a syncopated counterpoint to her wildly beating heart. The soft swish, swish of the leaves crushing in the yard, then the crunch, crunch on the gravel of the path to the door, then...

THUD!

against the door, rattling in its frame.

Felicity jumped, a small noise of fear in her throat. She heaved a shuddering breath and steeled herself, gathering her nerve.

"It's time you got yourselves home to bed, ain't it?" she

called out into the night. She padded her way to the front door, grabbing the axe from its home next to the door. Fortified now by her weapon, Felicity reached out and opened the door slowly, just a crack, so she could see if any tricksters were outside, perhaps throwing mud pies at the house like they had done last summer.

There, on the threshold, was no wayward child or mud pie. Instead, someone had left a large stone statue of a cat.

Felicity stood blinking for a moment. The statue was enormous. It stood as high as her shoulder. Felicity could see that the artist had chiselled flat, angular planes rather than curved ones to create the bulk of the image, with circular furrows for spots that may have been carved with some form of a compass. In the darkness, she could see that the creature's half-opened mouth sported sharp teeth that looked like a saw blade. In her imagination, Felicity could almost feel the effect of those teeth tearing through a trapped hand.

She peered into the blackness, thinking she might spy a fleet-footed prankster or hear the giggles of a pack of teens. But the yard seemed empty, the road silent.

How did the statue get here? It must have taken several large men to lift, and even then they would have required rollers to move it. She squeezed her way past it and looked into the empty street. The full moon hung overhead, showing a bright landscape to her dark-adjusted eyes. Nobody around.

"They've snuck 'round the side of the house," she thought to herself, and, holding the axe aloft like a brand, she gingerly made her way barefooted across the cold, dew wet grass. But as she rounded the corner, she saw nothing.

She walked around to the back of the house, checking that nobody was hiding, playing a bizarre prank, but the night was all quiet and nothing moved.

Felicity frowned. Faster now, she circled the entire house, searching all the while, then, her search fruitless, ran out onto the road, wildly swinging her gaze from one way to the next.

"Hooligans!" she cried out in anger, panting from her exertion. Grumbling her frustrations, she turned wearily toward the house.

Against the light that streamed from her open front door, she could clearly see that the statue was gone. The door stood open, as she had left it, but the cat was no longer there.

She looked around sharply, peering into the night.

"This ain't funny, ya piece of shite!" With false bravado, she held up the axe and lied, "I seen ya, and I know yer mam! I'll be speaking with her tomorrow about this!" Then she backed her way to the door, keeping her eyes on the street as long as she could before pulling it closed.

Turning, she let out an involuntary scream as she discovered the stone statue again. It was there, inside her house, facing toward the fireplace, away from the entrance. She took a step back, but the door coming to rest solidly behind her back gave her little comfort. Felicity brandished the axe in front of her like a sword. "Where are you?" she yelled, her voice falling flat against the walls of her tiny home. "Stay back! I have an axe, and if you don't show yerselves immediately, you'll get it, the lot of you!" But inside, she trembled, afraid to step further into her own domain.

Strangely, the statue looked different from this perspective, or was her mind playing tricks? She had thought the cat to be standing before, but now it was seated on its back haunches.

It didn't really occur to her in the heat of the moment that the size of the house precluded anyone from both showing themselves and staying back, especially with a large statue in the middle of the living space, but her reactions were far faster than her brain, which was slowly working out that this was a far more peculiar situation than a mere home invasion.

"What do you want?" she yelled into the room, at nobody.

So slowly she may have imagined it, the cat's head turned to look at her.

The fear was palpable now. Felicity felt a large lump in her throat, and she felt like air was barely reaching her lungs. As her breath came, faster and faster, she heard a strange buzzing in her ears, and her lips began to tingle. She stumbled toward the settee, feeling her heart trying to break its way through her ribs. Then grey clouded her vision and Felicity fainted to the floor.

She was breathing normally once more when she came to, but her lips were numb and her fingers stiff and frozen into crab-claws. Slowly she opened her eyes, and, for just a moment, her brain refused to translate the image before her. Then shapes reassembled themselves within her head and she found herself looking up at the stone cat who was, in turn, looking down at her. At some point in time, someone had draped a string around its neck with a small envelope tied to it. She found the sway of it hypnotic and stared at its to-ing and fro-ing for quite a few seconds before she realised she should move.

Shaky fingers reached up to grab the swaying envelope. With a slight tug, the string broke, and it came away from the cat's neck. Her prize now in hand, she rolled away from the statue and pushed herself into a sitting position.

The light from the dying coals was dim, but she could see the word "Felicity" written across the outer in a flowing, extravagant hand. Carefully, she ran the edge of her fingernail under the seal which held the flap down.

With a slight 'Pop!' the seal came away from the paper, and the note unfolded itself. The crisp sound of the parchment seemed unnaturally loud, and some instinct inside her tried to breathe quieter to offset the noise. Squinting in the barely-present light, Felicity moved further toward the fireplace to read. Suddenly, the eyes of the cat lit up — a bright, white light beaming straight ahead, bouncing off the plastered wall and lighting the entire (empty of other people) room.

Felicity blinked in the sudden light and lifted the letter with trembling fingers, while her eyes never left the statue. In the back of her brain she tried to make sense of the mechanism that turned the head, moved the limbs, but there were no hinges, no creases that might hide separate stone sections, no pivot points.

My Dear Felicity,

It is with the greatest sincerity that I thank you for the opportunity to work with your son Peter. I believe him to have a sharp mind and to carry a similar level of talent to his late father. Please accept this first payment as per our agreement. Do remember to separate Peter's portion from your own and keep it safe for him. I have provided a written copy of our agreement so that you can refer to it if in doubt of the portions.

I remind you that the contract has been declared thusly:

1. That I, Norman Linter, do undertake to apprentice Peter Diefen until the day, and hour, and second, of his eighteenth birthday.

2. That I, Norman Linter, will endeavour to clothe and feed Peter Diefen for the duration of his apprenticeship. In addition, I, Norman Linter, shall endeavour to keep Peter Diefen safe from harm to the best of my ability during this period of apprenticeship.

3. That Peter Diefen will do his utmost to defer and comply to all instructions given by me, Norman Linter, until the finalisation of his apprenticeship.

4. That I, Norman Linter, provide payment of 15 crowns per month as wage to Peter Diefen, for the duration of his apprenticeship, to be held in escrow by Felicity Diefen, and to be presented to Peter Diefen upon the day, and the hour, and the second, of his eighteenth birthday by Felicity Diefen.

5. That I, Norman Linter, provide payment of 5 Crowns per month to Felicity Diefen, as reimbursement for lost labour and as accountancy payment.

6. That this contract is magically enforced. Any breach to the terms of this contract will be balanced by the universe in a payment in flesh equivalent to the loss suffered by the aggrieved parties.

I do hope we have time to catch up and reminisce sometime soon.

With Deep Regard,

Norman.

P.S. Suzie bites. Please treat her kindly. She may not be able to talk, but she is highly intelligent — sometimes I think she is perhaps more intelligent even than myself.

Felicity blinked, looking blankly at the sheets of paper in her hand. Indeed, Norman had provided a written copy of their agreement, the numbers written in a vivid, almost iridescent purple to stand out from the black ink of the rest of the contract. What it all meant, though, was beyond her.

Felicity looked up from the page. Apart from the cat statue, she could see nobody.

"So," she said, looking around the room in the general direction of the statue, "Norman's paying me in stone carvings now? Where's this blasted Suzie that's supposed to be making a delivery? All this mucking around isn't funny. You'd better not be doing any of these hijinks in the future, I'll tell you that!"

A slight movement brought her attention back to the statue. The tongue, visible inside the open mouth, appeared to be a moving belt. From somewhere in the bowels of the statue, a row of shiny, golden coins smoothly ascended, dropping from the mouth one at a time to chink loudly onto the flagstones of the floor. Felicity bent to grab at them, counting as she went, until she had all twenty coins in hand.

Then, as suddenly as the light had come on, it went out, and Felicity was left in blackness, green afterimages playing in front of her eyes.

"Oi, that's not right! You can't just leave me in the dark.

What if I fall over and break me bloody neck? You're a menace, that's what you are."

By the time her eyes had adjusted to the darkness, Felicity was alone in the room. The stone cat was gone. Only the letter and the twenty coins in her hand stood as proof that the events of the evening were not a dream.

Through the night, Felicity lay awake and restless, a knot clenched in her belly. The thought of the large amount of money, now wrapped in a pouch and held tightly in her hand, made her feel unsafe. It was so long since she had possessed anything worth burgling that she didn't know what to do. Plans flitted through her mind; she could bury the gold, but she might be seen. She couldn't carry it, not long term; that small pile would soon grow beyond carrying. She could think of nowhere in her tiny home that would be safe from cunning thieves.

So she tossed and she turned, she rolled over again and again; she threw off her covers and she pulled them back on, and at every moment the weight of that coin pouch lay heavy upon her.

Come morning, she rose, exhausted and black-eyed. No solution had appeared to her in the dark, so she tied it securely to her waist, inside her clothing where nobody could see it. Still, even fully clothed, she felt as if the lump left by the pouch screamed its presence to the outer world.

Determined to show normalcy, she hung the shingle out that proclaimed she was open for business, then set herself down in her worn chair with the embroidery she had taken on only yesterday. But inside, she felt a brief smile at the thought of how much wood she could buy—enough to keep her through the winter, perhaps. Plans formed in her head of shopping, perhaps even to fill her larder. Later. When it was warmer.

She had barely completed the first petal of the rose she was stitching when the door opened. She looked up, her carefully practised smile for customers pasted onto her face. But the burly teen standing before her was not a customer. Felicity's smile grew wider, not in friendship, but in fear. She knew this man, Mick, and while she and his mother were on good terms, she and his employer were not. He looked unhappy.

"Why the long face, Mick," Felicity asked. "This morning's rain was enough to wet the flowers and green the grass, and now the sun is shining. Nobody should feel gloom on a day such as this."

"It's the first of the month," he growled in a deep, tired rumble. "With what you owed last month, we're now sitting at thirty-eight and two. I'm under instructions that if you can't pay fifteen, it's eviction."

She breathed a sigh of relief. "Oh, I can pay fifteen shilling, that's not going to be a problem..."

"Not silver, 'Liss, gold. He wants fifteen crown. I know you're struggling but Dingy Dunforth has said he's not extending any more credit and he needs you to pay the lot immediately. He says if you can't pay me I'm supposed to hurt you, but I don't want to do that."

Felicity froze. Her landlord had always allowed her leeway with her payments, knowing that her situation made it difficult to meet the monthly payments on the tiny home, but the debt had originally been to the late Mr Dunforth Senior. He had been kind to Felicity for a long time and had a lot of forgiveness in his heart, knowing as a widower how hard it was to raise a child alone. He had died just two months ago, and his son Dagney had taken over the accounts.

"It's not just you, 'Liss. It's everyone," Mick explained. "Some bad gambling debt or something, I suppose. He's calling it all in. There's a lot as are cold tonight. If you need a place for you and your boy..."

"You shouldn't call him names, Mick," Felicity warned. "People talk and if that name gets back to him you're going to have a hard time of it yourself. Mr Dunforth's name is Dagney, not… what you said."

Mick had the good sense to look ashamed. "Yes, Ma'am," he said, eyes downcast.

Mick was a good boy, truth be told. A few years older than Peter, and a solid boy, wide as he was tall. Dunforth had seized on the opportunity to mould this child into an enforcer, and the look was there, if not the temperament. Felicity hoped that Mick would remain as sweet as he was, but she feared that the work with Dagney would begin to warp the boy's sense of right and wrong.

Felicity took a deep breath and made a decision. "There's no need to fret over the boy; he has a roof. I've 'prenticed him to Norman Linter." Mick raised an eyebrow at this, but said nothing. "As for myself, hold tight a moment; we'll see what we can do over the money." Then, curtly, she turned and entered her small bedroom, shutting the door tight behind her. With trembling fingers, she pulled the pouch out from its concealment amongst her skirts and counted out the fifteen crowns demanded of her. With a shrinking heart, she placed the remaining five beneath her pillow.

Guilt ate at her as she opened the door, then passed the glinting pieces of metal to Mick. His mouth hung open as he counted each coin, then he solemnly wrote a receipt on a piece of paper. Felicity could see the emotions playing over Mick's face — astonishment, worry, guilt, regret, sadness, relief... they warred within him, and she felt a moment of pity for the bear of a boy who was now Dagney Dunforth's enforcer. She knew him for a gentle, kind-hearted child, and had difficulty reconciling that image with the one of Mick the bully-boy.

A short moment later, the coins were tucked into the small chest that attached to his belt, and the paper lay in Felicity's hand. His hand upon the doorknob, Mick turned to look deeply at Felicity.

"Miss Liss..."

But Felicity didn't want to hear the next words from his mouth. "Hush, Mick," she said gently, "Hie you home safely to your mam tonight, you hear? There are some as may be angry with your master's decisions today. Best do it early, to give them time to arrange other things. I have one small bed free for a child, if need be. Now get you gone; I've a gown to do."

He gave a last look back, then softly left, closing the door behind him. Felicity watched the back of the boy who was barely 15 and felt a small pang that she would miss out on seeing her son at this age, growing into his arms and legs, still a boy but becoming a man.

Felicity waited for a count of one hundred before cracking the front door again. Then, seeing that he was gone, she pulled in the shingle, gathered the remaining coins once more together, and left the house. The conditions of the contract ticked over in her mind, the numbers lodged in her throat and lying heavy in her gut as she walked steadily down the road, and it was some time before she realised that she had no idea where she was going. Only that she had to find Norman and Peter. She had to tell them what had happened.

The trees to either side of the road seemed never-changing and hypnotic. Her inward focus deepened, until she became so intent on the litany of self-reprisal and guilt that she barely noticed the forks in the road appearing then disappearing behind her, the choices made and irrevocable. Slowly, her surroundings became increasingly ominous, feeding the deep-seated terror that assailed her mind. On she trudged, hour upon hour, uncertainty and fear a roiling tornado in her mind.

Chapter 7

POWER

653 OM Tarandeer
Year of the Leaping Rabbit

Norman's Tower

Suzie moved to the window to look out of it. Norman, only a second before lost deep in the ancient text spread out before him, looked up in surprise. The cat normally saved its energy by remaining stock still, especially after trips like the one it had taken the night before. He carefully closed the book, then rose to see what had interested the gargoyle.

It was a while before he saw it—the tiny speck of movement. But there it was, snaking a trail across the land ever so slowly. Norman understood Suzie's interest now as he watched the road scour its way into the landscape. Only a few had that sort of power willingly on tap, and none that he knew would spend it so frivolously. But unwittingly? Yes. He knew who it must be.

Norman sighed and started making himself presentable. It wouldn't do to appear bedraggled in the presence of his impending houseguest. Then, hair neatened, clothing straightened, he stepped out and down the stairs in search of his charge.

Norman had few demands yet of Peter, preferring to allow him the chance to discover the secrets of the tower and its surrounds. Amongst those few tasks were the gathering of firewood, the hauling of water, and other small domestic chores, like washing clothes. However, this meant that, for the bulk of the day, the boy was nowhere to be seen.

The wizard closed his eyes and breathed in deeply. Waiting for the small, sharp, clean ache in the back of his nose that always reminded him (conflictingly) of winter and getting a noseful of water at the beach, he focussed on locating the bright flicker of the boy's life essence.

The boy remained unseen.

Frowning slightly, Norman peered harder, feeling the blazing form of Suzie, the smaller form of the wyrmling in the yard, the distant form of the traveller, the tiny sparks of birds, fish, insects... and there, almost a kilometre away, sneaking along amongst the oblivious alarm frogs, he felt the boy. It was faint, just a shadow of a form, but there he was.

Norman felt pride welling up inside of him that this boy, only two weeks into his apprenticeship, had already learned to hide himself from the eyes of others. Far from being a use of magic, this was a suppression of it, and a tool that few ever mastered. The boy truly was his father's son.

Then, eyes still closed, Norman waited for the smell of burning hair, acrid and pungent. The swift feeling of constriction around his chest prompted him then to open his eyes, and there stood the boy, his back to him, softly placing his foot into the water next to the large alarm frog only millimetres from his leg.

"Home, now," Norman said into the silence, and Peter was caught surprised and off balance. As he missed his footing, he came tumbling down, soaked, and the alarm frog was startled into peals of high-pitched warbling. Moments later, all the frogs nearby had started up their wail, making Norman's shouts impossible to decipher. But Peter had heard the message, and thinking himself in some sort of trouble, he hightailed it past the wizard towards the tower.

Felicity, tired and stumbling, heard the unearthly cries and hurried her pace, her heart beating frantically in her heaving chest. Her fears for herself abated and now she only felt fear for her son as visions of him being tormented by the creatures making the noise filled her mind. The more she thought of this, the more she hurried, until suddenly she was running.

Norman had been prepared to wander back at a leisurely pace, but a blast of wild magical energy rippling through the landscape rocked over him, leaving him with the cloying perfume smell of rotting roses filling his nose and making him feel sick to the stomach. The landscape warped around him, drawn in towards the source of the magic. The shadows deepened and seemed to reach for him with tendrilled fingers, subtly menacing. Sweat broke out on his brow and his stomach roiled as he fought the wave of fear crashing around him.

Closing his eyes, Norman attempted to teleport once more, but the scent of the wild magic surrounded him and refused to leave his nostrils.

The wizard frantically searched his pockets for something he could use. Then, finally, he found it. A single firestarter, wrapped tightly in its tattered red ribbon, covered in lint and sticky pocket-candy. With trembling hands, he pulled his knife from his belt and cut a fat lock of hair. Then, in a manoeuvre that he hadn't performed in many years, he lit the hair and breathed in the smell.

Felicity broke through to the field surrounding the tower and was greeted by the sight of Peter running like the hounds of hell were after him. She sprinted across the grass towards him, and as she reached him, a loud "boom" sounded from the direction he had come from. She grabbed him and covered him, desperate to protect him from any unseen assailants.

"Mum?" Peter asked, muffled in the folds of her dress.

"I should never have let you come here," she wailed with great, heaving sobs. "Not with that man. I should have known. Your father... he would be here today... he would be here for you... It's his fault... Your father's not here because of him..."

At the edge of the field, unable to move further into the maelstrom of wild magic that was erupting from Felicity, Norman listened, grief stricken.

Chapter 8

643 OM Tarandeer
Year of the Hunting Sparrow

Pugton

"She's going to be really annoyed that we're out," Gareth called to his friend. "She's been pacing and fussing for days now, and if I'm gone more than five minutes I get an earful."

Norman jogged to catch up with Gareth's long stride. "Yes, but you needed a break. Besides, adventure awaits! Soon you won't be able to even get this; you'll be chained to the cradle, making sure Liss doesn't go insane from lack of sleep."

"So, exactly like now then?"

Gareth's laughter filled the cavern they were currently exploring. Felicity, his wife of less than a year, was heavily pregnant and had become increasingly demanding as her belly grew.

Norman missed Gareth. Once, they had been inseparable — two apprentices knocking around, learning beside each other, and then when they'd both reached majority, moving together into an actual town, sharing a small place for convenience — until Felicity had dragged Gareth into settling down and getting a house to raise a family in. Now, Norman barely saw him. Finding this cavern had been a gift, and Norman had leapt at the chance to invite his friend on this picnic/exploration; a sojourn into the darkness.

"So, what do you think of my little toy?" Gareth asked, turning to face Norman as he continued to walk forward. "Perfect for camping trips. Liss always complains that the ground is too hard, so I can fit a couple of beds into that pavilion, drag around an entire larder, a bathtub. I've tinkered with the physics so the water will stay in the tub and there's heating available."

"It's interesting. Folds down to a wagon, I saw."

"It'll fold smaller than that if you really need it to. Pocket sized block. Folds into the dimensional cracks. I've even spread the mass load over a rough hectare so it's easy to lift."

Gareth reached into a fold of his tunic, drawing out a fist-sized grey cube and tossing it. Norman reached up a hand and caught it, fumbling a little when the cube turned out to be lighter than he expected.

"I made two. That one's my prototype, so it's got fewer features, but it's still good. Keep it. I'll show you how it all works — next week maybe — but today is just us!" Gareth hollered into the cave system, the echoes bouncing off the walls and back at them.

They walked together through the long cave, at times amazed at the immense space that opened above them, Gareth's light-bob floating up to illuminate the walls and roof at his mental command. The floor was smooth and clear of debris, as if animals had regularly walked this passage over the millennia since it had formed. Small plunks of water dripping into deep pools echoed at them whenever they stopped speaking, and Norman's heart swelled at the thought of his best friend there beside him.

Sometimes, Norman considered what the world might have been like if he were a girl. Gareth may have looked at him differently. Maybe they would be a couple rather than Gareth being with Felicity. Maybe Norman could have expressed his desires to the vibrant young man beside him. However, that ship had passed, and life had pushed Gareth in the direction of the young woman he had married. Norman was left with an aching pit of yearning in his chest and a resolve to keep himself close, to protect the blossoming family from anything that could cause them pain.

Coming to a wide, flat chamber with numerous openings, Norman took a deep breath in.

"What do you think, we set up for dinner here?" He pulled a tablecloth out of his backpack and shook it open. "Nice flat spot, probably no ants, romantic atmosphere…"

Gareth chuckled. It really was a nice spot. The roof was high, with striations of colour—pinks, yellows, reds. Small crystals had formed along some of the stalactites, and they bounced the light around the room in dazzling spots that moved whenever the light-bob moved.

"What did you bring us to eat," Gareth asked. He swiped a hand over his light brown hair to push it out of his eyes. "I could eat an entire horse, I think."

"Nothing too grand," Norman said airily, as he first pulled crockery and cutlery from a pocket of his pack, then nonchalantly lifted out a steaming pan of roast beef. A platter of roasted root vegetables. A large bowl of steamed greens. A shepherd's pie…

One after another, dishes filled the cloth. First, savoury items and sauces, then sweeter food, pastries, creamy chilled flans, fruit platters, all lifted from a small, flat pocket on his pack.

"You don't think you may have prepared a little too much for just the two of us, then?" Gareth's voice had just a touch of sarcasm, but it was laced with fondness. Then his voice softened. "This is good. I needed the space. This is good."

As predicted, the picnic was free of ants. The two men chatted amiably, discussing techniques they had discovered and brainstorming new ideas to try.

"I see your pockets have increased in number," Gareth nudged. "Still got the old 'sniff test' going?"

"It's an annoying sense trigger to have," Norman grumbled. "How do you replicate the smell of a rainy day? But I got hold of an apothecary in Bakar and she's going to distil some oils for me, get a good range of fruits and flowers, maybe some herbs. I should be able to lose some of the bulk then and switch to something more compact." He reached into a pocket near his waist, pulled out a whole lemon, gave it a deep sniff, then waved the piles of leftover food and dirty plates to the dimensional pocket on his backpack.

"You should draw. It's so much easier — I just put a pad in my bag and a stick of charcoal and away I go!" Gareth mimed the motion of a pencil in the air, writing an invisible ode into the space around him.

Norman rolled his eyes. Gareth sometimes failed to understand that he couldn't just switch to a more convenient sense trigger.

"What do you do in an emergency? Whip out your pad and draw while your house is burning around you? Face it, your method is slow. There are trade-offs to consider."

"Pff, you with your hundreds of pockets, you think you're better?"

Norman pouted. "It's not hundreds, it's forty, and some of them are empty." He patted his floppy right breast pockets for emphasis.

The look on Gareth's face said to Norman that he had just proven his point, especially when Norman realised the pocket he had just patted had a lump of pine resin nestled in one corner. "Oh! I've been looking for that..."

Having stowed all their gear away, the two men started walking once more. Choosing a new, random direction, they stepped off into a dark tunnel, followed closely by Gareth's light bob. The path branched, and branched again, sometimes wide and echoing, sometimes narrowing so that the men had to squeeze sideways through the gaps, and sometimes the ceiling lowered so the men were forced to stoop. The clutter of rubble increased around them, but still a small path wended its way around the boulders and stalagmites.

"What's that?" Gareth pointed to a wall where discolourations appeared to break the layers of sediment. The light bob drifted forward at Gareth's mental command, above and ahead of them so their shadows would fade from the rockface.

There, in the varied hues of ochre, chalk, and charcoal, were crude pictures of two-legged beings chasing animals. Looking for more signs, they could see that the pictures extended further along the passageway, beyond the reach of the light, into the darkness in both directions.

Gareth flipped a second light bob from his pocket. "That looks like a picture of a portal," he said, pointing to a space further away. "I'm going to check it out. Can you see any other uses of magic back the way we came?"

The second light bob wove its way to Norman, who started studying the wall in earnest. The ancient pictures were crumbly and dust had settled into the imperfections in the surface, making the images hard to make out. Dragons appeared alongside winged humanoids, people on two legs pointed sticks at animals or other people, crudely drawn charcoal trees burned in red ochre fires.

Norman turned to call out his findings to Gareth, but the sound died in his throat as he saw a creature trundle into view at the edge of Gareth's light. It was long and slow, looking somewhat like a smooth, wet lizard. Its glistening skin was red, with paler orange spots that glowed faintly, visible even in the darkness.

"Gareth," he whispered hoarsely to his friend, who appeared immersed in the contents of the picture before him. "Gareth…"

The thing came further into view, its head shaped like the broad head of an arrow. Milky eyes were set low into the sides of its head, with bulbous lumps behind them that looked to be oozing some sort of clear fluid. With a start, Norman realised he was looking not at a lizard but a salamander; to be specific, a greater spotted fire-salamander. While blind to everything except changes in light and not typically aggressive, Norman had read that they were quite dangerous.

He crept forward, trying to reach Gareth silently to alert him to the danger, when his unsuspecting friend suddenly turned to move further down the corridor and tripped, falling headfirst onto the creature. The startled animal opened its wide mouth and hissed, flaps on the side of its head unfurling in a frill and directing those bulbous lumps to exude oily gel onto what it could only have thought was a predator.

"Oh, shit," said Gareth, climbing onto his knees and wiping the thick, faintly orange exudate from his eyes. "What's that?"

More gel shot from the salamander's poison glands, coating Gareth's torso as he wiped his hands on his pants.

"Get back here," yelled Norman, scared for his friend but uncertain how to proceed. "Get away from that thing!"

"Oh, shit," said Gareth again, stumbling toward Norman while staring at his hands, "I'm feeling weird. This is getting hot." Norman ran to his friend, watching in horror as Gareth's skin reddened and blistered wherever the ooze lay, then started breaking into small flames.

Without dropping his eyes from Gareth, he reached for a pocket at his left breast to grab a pinch of powder and while concentrating in the direction of his friend, let a stream of magic flow as he snorted the powder deep into his sinuses.

Too late, he realised that the powder was not the dry, red dirt that would trigger a flow of fresh water. Instead, a gout of searing flame leapt toward his friend, triggered by the cedar ash that had been in the next pocket along.

The salamander rushed towards the bright light, excited at the prospect of a freshly cooked meal. Mouth open wide, it grabbed ahold of Gareth's still-burning leg with a strong bite, gripping the muscle with its small, conical teeth. With a toss of its head, Gareth's entire calf ripped from the bone and the salamander moved backwards to chew on the large piece of meat.

Gareth screamed hoarsely, flame licking down his throat until the sound changed to noiseless gurgles. His clothing burned away, patches of white or red skin showing clearly beside the blackened and charred surface of his face and neck.

Fumbling, Norman spilled his pockets onto the ground, scrabbling for the red dirt. Focusing his gaze onto the ground before him, he picked a pinch from the tiny pile in trembling hands, brought to his nose, and inhaled sharply.

Water engulfed him in a globe as he moved to his friend to douse the flames. Unbreathing, he felt the water bubble and boil around him as he took Gareth in his arms, then when not a trace of the searing heat remained, he released his hold on the magic.

Gareth was unmoving.

Norman held his friend, cradling his head, kissing his hair. It smelled acrid, pungent, unforgettable, as the young artificer's breath rattled with each gasp, trying to take in air that was all around but could not reach his lungs.

"No, Gareth, no, no," Norman moaned. "We'll fix you. A doctor. We need a doctor." His mind flashed over who would be most capable of help, all the while struggling not to think of Felicity and how she would react. Panic flooded through him as he realised that he had no way of getting Gareth to the surface, and he wasn't even sure he could find his way back through the labyrinth of passages.

With the smell of his friend's burning hair in his nostrils, something happened that had never happened before. Unthinkingly, Norman's panic reached a peak, and suddenly he was in a strange room being stared at by a panting, red-faced Felicity lying on her back and her elderly midwife standing in the middle of the room, holding onto a steaming towel.

"He needs help. Please. Anything!" Norman screamed at the midwife.

The woman patted Felicity's knee. "You just relax there —

you've plenty of time yet. I'll take a look at this.

"Put him down on the other bed there. Don't mind that it's rumpled—it's mine."

Norman barely noticed his surroundings as he gently placed Gareth's trembling body onto the bed. Static played loudly in his ears and he could feel his pulse shaking his body as his brain looped the image of Gareth on fire behind his eyes.

"Who is that, Norman?" Felicity asked from the bed on the other side of the room.

He stared at her, wide-eyed.

"Norman? Are you okay? Who is that?" Felicity repeated.

His pulse thrummed in his veins, a distinctive beat pushing his torso, a firm 'Your. Fault. Your. Fault. Your. Fault.' playing in his head. He tried to speak past the stone in his throat—it felt so large that he thought he might never be able to swallow again. He looked into the eyes of Gareth's wife, who in hours would be the mother of Gareth's child, and the stone rose, trying to disgorge itself from his body.

He turned and ran through the door, out of the house, stopping briefly in the garden to vomit the rich meal he had eaten just an hour before, before running unseeing until he found himself at a stone corner post, staring up at the tower house he had built for the four of them—a surprise he had planned so that they could all stay together.

Hot tears ran down his face as he pounded his fists into the stone, over and over again, the anger at himself rising, increasing, until it reached a peak and he screamed at himself, wanting to be far from everyone and everything, throwing his fist against the stone as hard as he possibly could, hearing the bones in his knuckles crack.

He slumped to the ground, great sobs shaking his body, as the building settled into place in its new location, far from the town it had been in yesterday.

Chapter 9

661 OM Tarandeer
Year of the Tangled Briar

Norman's Tower

Petunia woke slowly and with a lot of groaning. Peter had moved them both to sit on the side of his bed, cushioning the small body in the soft folds of his quilt, and this is where she found herself.

"Why are you wet?" The first words issuing from her mouth were muzzy and her tongue felt like it filled her mouth.

Peter turned his face immediately to her and she noted red eyes.

"Whatever it is, it's okay. We'll get you through it," she said blearily. Then, with a flash, she remembered the events of the morning.

"Why am I here? Where's Norman? There's a fire! We need to go! IT'S GONE! WE NEED TO GO! WE NEED TO GET…"

"Shh," Peter put a hand gently over her trembling wings. "You knocked yourself out because you were panicking. Don't start panicking again. 'A clear head is best when the whole world is stressed.'" Peter's imitation of one of Norman's frequent sayings made Petunia giggle, and with that she felt less rushed.

"The fire is out. It seems I'm good at moving a lot of water now. I could have done with that a decade ago… it would have saved a lot of trudging up and down stairs with buckets. And Norman isn't here right now; I don't know where he is. It's a bit of a worry, but this is where we are. Now, slowly and with as much explanation as you can give, what's gone and where do we need to go?"

Petunia closed her eyes and thought back to the morning's discovery. "I was doing my morning count and my silver coin wasn't there. My wire, my brass fittings, my chain… everything's still where I left it except for my coin. It's been stolen. The mean boy took it. We need to go get it from him because he's horrible and he can't just steal my hoard."

Peter frowned. "That sounds bad. It's not okay that he's taken anything of yours. Of course we'll go and get it back. Now, who is this mean boy and how do we find him?"

"I know where he lives. He lives near where your mum lives. We should go there and take it off him."

Peter was relieved that Petunia had given him clear instructions. He felt very off-centre without Norman around to tell him what to do. He still wasn't certain how or why this strange person had stolen a piece of Petunia's hoard out from under her, but today was turning out to be an odd one so he decided not to question her further about it.

"Well, let's get Suzie and we'll go. Do you want me to lock up the rest of your hoard so it's safe from more thieves?"

Petunia hadn't considered further theft, so she nodded emphatically. This, unfortunately, caused her to become dizzy, perhaps a byproduct of her earlier head trauma. "Could you get them all for me? I'm still not feeling good."

With a smile, Peter assented, and took a small wooden box out to the charred remnants of Petunia's bush. Sifting through the ash and soil, he gathered up the now cool pieces of metal and deposited them in the box. Giving a last sweep, he moved his hands out in a wider circle to make certain he hadn't missed anything. He was glad he had as he scooped up a final small coin a little further from the other hoard pieces, black from its thick covering of soot, and dropped it into the box. With a smile, he dropped the lid on the box and locked it with a thought. Nothing would be able to make it through that spell, short of the box's destruction.

Packing the box away in the bottom of his clothes chest, he reassured the tiny dragon. "I checked all over and got all of the metal. Everything is safe inside the box, and the box is packed away with my socks. Nobody is going to be searching my socks for valuables. Especially not those socks."

Chapter 10

661 OM Tarandeer
Year of the Tangled Briar

Atinien Mountain

Albert's bedroom reeked of urine. Where the house had been pristine to this point other than a light coat of dust, this room was in need of the less-than-tender ministrations of a hearty and heartless cleaner.

With an arm supporting Albert, Norman pivoted and moved to the rarely used lounge area.

"Take the settee for a short while," he said. "I just need to set your bedroom to order."

Stripping the bed of its sheets and blankets near overpowered Norman with the smell of ammonia. The straw-filled mattress was soaked through — in some places black with mould, in others green as the moisture had sprouted stray seed. The bed frame seemed to be unaffected, so with as little contact as possible, Norman dragged the mattress into the centre of the room.

The chamber pot beside the bed was filled to the brim. It was obvious that Albert had been unable to visit the outdoor facilities for a few days, perhaps lacking the strength to brave the cold outside.

Thinking for a few seconds, Norman decided that the bedroom was no longer fit for his mentor to reside in. Drawing from his sense memory, he imagined the scent of cedar ash. A sizzle started within the mattress, a bright orange glow licking at the fabric, spreading to the surrounding straw, oxidising each molecule within the mattress in turn. He drew oxygen through the various flues in the cave system, fuelling the flame until there was little left but a greasy, black residue where the mattress had once been. As an afterthought, he included the soiled sheets and blankets, burning them until no trace remained.

Then, funnelling the freshened air towards his face to create a barrier from the foul odours emanating from the contents of the chamber pot, he carefully lifted it and carried it down the long hallway to the frozen wasteland outside.

Having disposed of the waste and thoroughly cleaned the antique porcelain, he stepped into the now clean and aired room. Whispering a brief apology to the universe, he pulled from an unseen corner of the world. A pristine, down-filled mattress appeared, with deep pillows atop it and fresh, folded, bright white, linen sheets.

He may have been frail, but Albert noticed the change the instant he was shifted into the freshly made bed.

"What rich bastard did you steal this from, eh?" he asked. "I'm glad you chose quality. I'd hate to be putting out someone who couldn't afford to replace their mattress."

"Don't worry, it's from a spare room at the Delingaard Imperial Palace. They can afford its loss."

Albert raised an eyebrow. "Ah, but can the poor servant who is set to clean that room? Not to mind. So long as it's not a regular occurrence, boy-o. I'd hate to think I raised a thief."

Having reassured his mentor about his ethical stances, Norman left for the kitchen. Finding little other than some old turnips and carrots stored in a box of sand, and the mushroom box in the corner picked mostly bare, he again apologised to the universe (mostly for the damage to the ears of forest creatures) and gathered ingredients. Apples from Falan, rosemary from Celwyn, wild spinach from Jerros... the list grew until he had filled the benches with fresh ingredients. Finally, he sent his mind ranging until he found a rabbit, dead of heart failure only minutes before, that appeared to be parasite free. Rabbit stew, it was.

With the stew prepared and bubbling, Norman dragged the old, brass tub into the centre of the room. Water may have been in plentiful supply in this space — moving snow from outside to inside was easy enough — but the ambient temperature being as low as it was, Norman settled himself down to boil a large cauldron of water the old-fashioned method. He supposed this was one of the reasons Albert had built his home here; being forced to do things without magic was in some ways quite calming. A watched kettle gives a soul plenty of time to think.

"Have you had anyone else here since I was here last?" Norman asked over the small dining table.

Albert had cleaned up nicely and he was now dressed in fresh bedclothes, his hair combed, his beard bouncy and full again. His hands trembled as he lifted his spoon, but he was sitting upright, which Norman saw as a good sign.

"Eh? Anyone else? I'm too old to be worrying about other people coming and mucking up my things. No, I go to the council once every year. I have a couple of markets I get my supplies from. Other than that, I'm happy just to stay here and tinker."

"You need someone here with you. Get an apprentice."

"I'm done with apprentices, boy-o. You're my last. I'm not going to be here long enough to see another apprentice done."

Norman had not really been prepared to hear the finality in Albert's voice. He started to clutch at any hope he could muster.

"Then we'll have to shift you somewhere closer to people. We can't have you falling over and nobody being around to help…"

Albert grabbed firmly to the edges of the table. "You are not taking me anywhere," he blazed. "This is my home, I dug it myself, I have lived here for almost 600 years. I have outlived three wives, 17 children, all of my grandchildren, great-grandchildren, great-great-grandchildren… I couldn't tell a descendant if I was face to face with one. I have seen my proteges grow old and die. Who do I have left? You. You and a bunch of banal old men who think that living a long time means they know how to run things. You need to let me go. Do you remember the last time a seat on the council changed hands? No, you don't, because you hadn't been born yet. It's time for me to go.

"I'll tell you something not many know, but there's an age requirement for that council. You can't be elected if you're more than 70 years old. We need some young blood, so I'm tipping my hat for you. You've always been… progressive.

"But I'm staying here. It's not going to be too much time. I feel like it may be only a few days." His voice started to slow and his erect posture started to slump noticeably. "And now I'm tired. That tirade took it out of me. Can you help me to bed? I don't think I can make it by myself."

Norman stood and gently helped his aged mentor, one slow step at a time. Albert was panting and sweaty by the time they reached the bedroom, and he rolled into the bed with a groan.

"Please, Norman, I want to die here. Don't take me away from my family. Bury me with them. There is a door down to the mausoleum in the back of my wardrobe. Best place to hide it. Apprentices never try to poke at my clothing. And the succession box is in the wardrobe too. Best to set it for tomorrow. They can take the lodge. Hasn't been occupied for 90-odd years, but if a bunch of mages can't make do, what good are they?"

As Albert Tarandeer, Magus of the Council of Varthien, slept, each breath rattling in his chest, Norman watched, considered what he had just been told and flipping a small coin over in his pocket.

The succession box looked ordinary. A plain wooden cube with a leather hinge. But opening it up, he smelled the roast mutton that accompanied Albert's summons magic and he heard the chime—less intensely than others would hear due to his proximity to the source. Then he sat back and waited for the respondents to trickle in.

Chapter 11

627 OM Tarandeer
Year of the Stooping Raven

Sharpstone Manor

Norma sat in the dirt, looking at the boys. They had dissuaded Norma's efforts to join them, but they couldn't stop the slip of a child from following after them at a distance, watching them, copying what they did.

Norma's long, frilly skirts were pulled up between grimy legs and tucked into the waistband at the front in an imitation of the pants the boys wore. The delicate shoes that Mama insisted that "proper girls" wore had long been discarded and bare feet today, as most days, reigned. There would be repercussions for these minor acts of defiance—perhaps slightly harsher than normal considering the long tear in the bleached white underskirt that had occurred not ten minutes ago, but Norma didn't really mind. There would be no switch to the ass, like the boys would receive, nor cane across the palm; there was some amount of pleasure in being confined to the apartments, where solitary 'prayer and studies' meant that Norma would be left to think.

Mama had no patience with trying to instruct Norma in the

art of embroidery, whose fingers were always grimy and left prominent brown marks on the linen so that not even samplers were fit for display. Besides, Norma was prone to fidgeting when others required stillness, loudness when others required quiet, activity when others demanded senescence. And so Norma's days were mostly unfettered, except for days like today, when household duties required attendance because of guests.

The boys had stopped to look at something on the road. When one reached out with a stick, Norma surmised that it must be some small creature, run over by one of the wagons that ran to and fro for strange purposes unfathomable to the child.

Vaguely, Norma noted the sound of the bells ringing the hour. How dull it must be for Harald, sitting around waiting to tell people the time, Norma mused. Then, with a jolt, Norma realised that there was somewhere important to be, and with full speed, skirts were hiked up to the waist and legs pumped to get their owner back to the manor house as quickly as they could move.

Norma raced inside, door banging, but came to an abrupt stop as a bundle of soft grey linen blocked the path. The linen appeared to be draped loosely over a thin man with long, white hair and beard. He looked frail, a crooked back and just as crooked a stick holding him up, the grey robes drooping as if they had been tailored for a larger, taller man. Eight-year-old Norma noted that the hem was ratty and dirty, as if always trailing in the dust, and the man's bare toes peeped out, almost black from accumulated dirt.

Norma's mind twisted and tangled with glee, noticing the trail of muck the man's feet and robes were making on Mama's pristine floors, when a shrill voice cut through the air like a whip. "Norma! What on earth have you done to your gown? Get it out from between your legs at once. Refined women do not tuck their skirts up between their legs. Nor do they roll around in the pigsty, as I can only presume you have been doing to get your hair in such a state. Get Jenna to scrub you down at once; I expect you clean and presentable for our guests immediately."

Norma ducked instinctively, anticipating the customary clip around the ear, but this time Mama saved her ire for words rather than deeds, perhaps because of the seemliness of the occasion. Then he ran for the stairs, but not before he caught the old man's words in a voice like breath through a reed pipe; "Cheeky looking lad, that one. Out scampering with the other boys, I suspect. Norman, did you say his name was? Don't scold him too hard. Our childhood is only a mote in the eye of time; you should not begrudge him the enjoyment of it..."

A thrill coursed through the child, like an entire hive of bees buzzing inside Norma's chest. The man thought she was a he! Norma, now determined to be Norman, tried hard to hear how Mama responded, but whatever it was, it became unintelligible as the parlour doors closed. Later, after Jenna had attacked him first with scrub brush, then hairbrush, then with mountains of fabric that purported to be a dress, and he joined the evening's extravagance, he concluded that his mother had dared not contradict the old man. He was someone of some importance, the once-girl decided, because everyone in the vast room paid him deference with trailing eyes, hushed tones, and slight bows wherever he went. When Norman was presented, the man knelt down to his level.

"Ah, the young scamp has returned! Bah! Look at these silly ruffles they've got you wearing, m'boy. How's a lad supposed to go tadpole fishing wearing so many layers?"

"She's a terror!" Mama said beside them with a glass of something bubbly in her hand. "Tadpole fishing is the least of it. I'll never find her a good match."

The grey man looked him up and down. "Show me your teeth, boy," he commanded, and Norman happily grimaced bared teeth at him. He grabbed Norman's arm and felt for the muscles that were barely there.

"Do you have your letters, boy?"

Norman nodded.

"Yes, I think he'll do. I'll take him. How much do you

want?"

Mama's eyes widened. "Oh, I don't know if it's appropriate…"

"Not appropriate? 'Never find him a good match,' that's what you said. You've given up already. Whereas I need a boy to fetch and carry, and this one seems adequate to the task. My offer is this: He'll get 15 crown per month, you'll get 2, plus the social renown of being able to say your child is apprenticed to the Magus. I'll keep him until his majority, at which stage he'll have a profession, a nest egg, and prospects! Choice in whatever life partners he sees fit, from whatever land he sees fit, and whatever social strata he wishes."

Norma studied Mama's face as all this was being said, and he saw her wavering. Then her eyes dropped to Norman's hands, which were, as always, brown with the grime that never seemed to scrub out, with black crescents under each fingernail. Her gaze hardened.

"Sold," was her only word.

After the party had burned down to sputters of talk and sparks of tired laughter, a dozy Norman was lifted in a pair of arms and placed onto a warm, velvety surface, and a woollen blanket laid over him. He vaguely heard doors opening and closing, and muttered voices built palaces of dream within his head. When the gentle sway of the carriage started, he was rocked into a deep sleep.

He awoke in a new place, the hunched back of the grey man pottering over a kitchen stove, filling his nose with delicious smells.

"That mother of yours thinks I'm addled," the man said, without looking around. "Thinks I can't tell boys from girls. But it's her whose vision is faulty. She can't see the man you'll grow to be — too fixated on things that dangle or don't.

"My name is Albert. I don't like to be called 'Master', but it's customary, so you should probably call me 'Master' when other people are around. At all other times, I'm just Albert.

"This is your new home. I wasn't really expecting to pick up an apprentice, but I couldn't leave you to get buried in societal expectations. That's how we lose some of our brightest. So, I haven't carved out a bedroom for you yet, but give me a day or two and you'll have your own space.

"The mark on your wrist is a magemark. I think you were too tired last night to actually remember the contract, but it wouldn't have taken if you weren't completely willing. It will disappear when you turn eighteen. In the meantime, there are some perks it offers you, and you'll be mostly safe from untoward things happening."

Norman looked at his wrist. There, like it had been drawn on in ink, was a deep red-brown circle with a sigil inside that he didn't recognise.

"You're going to be a wizard, boy. I can feel it inside of you. It's a dragon fighting to scratch its way out of you. Do you feel it?"

Norman nodded. "Yes sir... um... Albert. It tickles in my nostrils."

"And before we go any further, are you okay with me calling you Norman? I don't want to presume, and if you've got another name you're more comfortable with..."

"Norman's good," he blurted, "And thank you. Nobody ever noticed that I was a boy before. It feels better."

Chapter 12

661 OM Tarandeer
Year of the Tangled Briar

Pugton

Felicity was eating morning tea when a strange chime pinged in her ear and a voice spoke.

"Succession within the Council of Mages has been called. All who possess magic are welcome to witness succession at Atinien Mountain lodge hall. Mages eligible for consideration will receive a complementary portal for 24 hours to attend, with guaranteed return to their original location for a further 24 hours."

Against the wall on the far side of the room, a light outlining an archway appeared, followed by the interior of the arch changing to look out on a snowy mountain scene, slightly tinged yellow with the occasional pinprick of yellow light sparkling across the face.

The half-eaten caramel tart stopped in front of her face as she took the scene in, wide-eyed. Her heart began to flutter with the shock of realisation that she was 'eligible for consideration'.

I'm not a mage, she thought. *Magic is horrid. I don't want to be a mage.*

She took a deep breath in, then let it out slowly. "You don't exist," she told the portal firmly. "I don't care what you want. I'm going out."

She placed the caramel tart back on the small plate in front of her, gathered her purse and hat, and left through the large doors of her pavilion.

Chapter 13

653 OM Tarandeer
Year of the Leaping Rabbit

Norman's Tower

Amidst the maelstrom, the child stroked his mother's shoulder gently.

"It's okay, Mum. I'm here. You're fine. It's okay..."

Over and over again, like a mantra, the boy repeated those words in a role reversal, taking care of the adult, soothing her. In just minutes, the wind had died down and Norman could breathe clearly again, no longer oppressed by the wild magic scent of rotting roses.

Peter continued to murmur soothing noises to Felicity as Norman approached, and reaching her side, she looked up at him, heaving great, trembling sobs.

"Norman, I... I'm not quite sure how I got here..."

"Let's go inside," he said, offering her a hand up, and she looked around at the sparse exterior.

"Wait, I recognise... Do I recognise this place?"

Norman inhaled sharply at the brief flash of painful memory. "Yes. I built it for all of us..." He stopped, swallowing hard. "I built it so we could all stay together. That night, when everything happened…"

Felicity was running her fingers over the stone, tracing the wide cracks that had formed when the building had teleported so many years ago.

"I always thought there had been a lightning strike," she said in wonder. "You moved an entire building? Why?"

"It wasn't intentional," he whispered. "The smell was so heavy. It was all I could smell. I was just so…"

"I never blamed you, you know. Not really. I knew you would never do that on purpose. I just said that earlier because I was upset and scared." Her breathing steady now, she turned to Norman. "Have you somewhere I can wash up? My face is starting to feel a bit stiff."

The three walked inside together.

"A bit sparse, isn't it?" Felicity asked, referring to the lack of internal walls.

Norman laughed, breaking the tension that had built up inside him. "Yes, I suppose it is. I never finished — I was waiting to surprise you and Gareth and ask you how you wanted the space to be divided up. A floor for me, two floors for the both of you and the baby. I never had the chance."

"And then you disappeared. You didn't even come back for his funeral."

"I was there, I just didn't want to intrude." Norman touched a quizzical Peter on the shoulder. "Can you fix some water for your mother to wash up with? And maybe put a kettle on for some tea? Your mother and I have some things we need to talk about."

Peter nodded, grateful for something to do, and ran upstairs for a bowl. Norman and Felicity ascended the stairs at a more sedate pace as the child ran back down past them, heading out to the well for its cool, clear water.

Over the next hour, Norman recounted the tale of that final, fateful day to Felicity. Then, she discussed the issue of debts that Gareth had left behind, the bills that she had failed to ever get on top of, right up to her current issue.

At some point, Peter had drawn a seat up beside them, and as Felicity spoke about taking from his portion of the money, he put a small hand on her knee.

"That's okay, Mum. If you need to use my money, do it. I don't mind."

Norman looked worried. "To a point, that's alright, but you need to make certain that you don't overdraw on his funds too often, and it all needs to be paid back by his eighteenth birthday. That's important."

Felicity breathed a huge sigh of relief. "Thank goodness. I was afraid something horrid would happen to me."

Norman smiled, pulling her into a hug. "I wish I had known about the debts earlier. I would have helped you." He looked across at Peter. "He looks so much like Gareth, doesn't he?"

There was a moment's silence, then Norman asked, "Gareth's things. Do you still have them somewhere?"

"Yes,", Felicity said slowly. "Not his clothing — it all got cut down to make Peter's clothing, but all of his tools and other things — they're in a basket at home. Why?"

Norman refused to tell her, preferring to wait until he had seen what was there. Pulling out the wagon, he called out to Suzie, who was rolling around on the newly created 'road' like a house cat. "Suzie, would you like to go for another trip to Pugton? You'll get to check out this new pathway Felicity has kindly made for you!"

Suzie uncharacteristically bounded up to Norman, nodding with a toothy smile.

"Okay everyone, we're going into town, and…" he looked at Peter, "…hopefully I can make the world a bit easier on your mum."

Chapter 14

661 OM Tarandeer
Year of the Tangled Briar

Norman's Tower

"Suzie, we need you," Peter called up the stairs.

Suzie considered ignoring him for a moment, but the boy was bound to get into trouble without supervision. She was feeling lively after the full meal she had eaten, so she wasn't at all perturbed by the sudden demand on her energy. Looking over at the ring on the floor, she was satisfied it was still pumping out magic and she could go back to feast as much as she wanted later. With an internal sigh, she shifted her form past the door (which Peter had left standing wide open earlier—hmph. Untidy.) and down the staircase that spiralled down the outer wall of the tower.

The boy, it seems, had called up the stairs and then left, expecting her compliance. As she reached the bottom of the stairs she could see the front door stood wide, Peter's back visible in the courtyard, tapping his foot. He had set up the wagon. Ugh. Beast of burden time. No please, no thank you, just an expectation.

She considered turning around to climb to the workroom

again, but Albert had asked her to look after Peter. With another inward sigh, she steeled herself to the task and walked up to the wagon, settling herself down between the yoke shafts. It bothered her a little that Peter had come to see her as little more than transportation, but she consoled herself with the recollection that he had but a week left of this apprenticeship, after which she would get Norman to herself once more.

Peter seemed preoccupied, chattering away to the young dragon while he connected the wagon. Only when he had climbed up onto the driver's seat did he direct his attention to her.

"We're headed into town, Suzie. Ready to go."

No manners. Hmph. She was sure he used to be more polite when he was younger, less inclined to assume her servitude. She glared at him through the stone on the back of her head, but he didn't notice. Probably because her artist hadn't put eyes there, and everyone seemed to expect that her vision was dependent on the shapes carved into her form.

She debated the speed at which she would take the path—on the one hand, dawdling would show her displeasure, but on the other hand speed would get her back home to that delicious ring more quickly. She decided to dawdle. Her calculations suggested the kinetic energy requirements would be greater if she used haste, and it would be poor precedent to waste energy just because she had it. At least the path was less difficult than it used to be, she considered. Ever since Felicity's brush with wild magic, a smooth, almost glassy road had become fused into the landscape, leading directly to the town.

Felicity was a strange one, Suzie mused. Afraid of everything, incapable of acting, causing herself difficulty by her own actions and then being incapable of understanding her own faults. If she were not so blitheringly incompetent, she might have made a halfway decent mage, but she had been so fixated on becoming nothing more than a wife and mother that those talents had lain fallow. Suzie had tried to get her head around the issue of Felicity for many years now. It remained a puzzle to her why anyone would choose to not develop their magic. She could not, however, fault the effect of the straight path that scarred the terrain, even though Norman found it bothersome that people could now easily come to call upon him.

Peter's talents must have arisen from the combined talents of methodical Gareth, an architectural wizard, and ineffectual Felicity, a woman too scared of her own shadow to begin to harness her own power. So, engineer Peter focussed his attention into his hands rather than his power, insisting on mundane solutions and inadvertently locking away his more esoteric talents. Such a waste, thought Suzie, not for the first time.

The things he created had a residual magical charge, showing that there was a trickle of flow, but that was barely more than the natural order—a slight strengthening of the bonds between objects so they needed less maintenance, like that water-carrier he jerry-rigged when he was just 12. It should have fallen apart just hours after it was created, rather than holding up for years, with only one piece of string needing to be replaced last year. Barely any flavour in that system. What use was that to her?

Suzie's train of thought was momentarily broken as Petunia fluttered her way onto a stony shoulder and gave the gargoyle a tiny hug.

"I love you, Suzie. Thank you for taking us to town."

Then Petunia flew back to Peter, her train of conversation unstoppable.

Perhaps it wouldn't hurt to move a little more quickly.

Chapter 15

FORGOTTEN BOXES

"I was saving these for Peter," Felicity said, pulling a heavy basket down from the rafters. "I suppose I could have given them to him at any time, but at first he was so young, and then it just never came up. I don't know what half of this stuff does anyway."

She reached in and started pulling things out, an item at a time, and lining them up neatly on the table. Peter looked with interest at the hammers, saws, chisels, and other tools that appeared.

"I can make things?" he asked, excited. "Like real things?"

Norman nodded in his direction, then scanned the minutiae in the basket that hadn't been removed yet.

"Aha!" he cried, reaching deep into the basket to pull out a white cube that gleamed like polished marble. "This is exactly what I was searching for."

"That kind-of looks like the wagon when it's folded down," said Peter, "just smaller and a different colour."

"You're right, Peter. This is precisely like the wagon, but it's better." He lifted his head to meet Felicity's eyes. "Are you completely in love with living in this house?"

Felicity looked taken aback. "Um… what?"

"I still own the land I originally built my tower on," he said as way of explanation, but Felicity and Peter both continued to stare at him in confusion. "Come for a walk and I'll show you."

Down the lane, around the corner, closer to the interior of town, they walked for less than five minutes before stopping in front of a tangle of thick grass and thorny bushes.

"Here!" he cried out in glee. "What do you think?"

Silence and stares met his beaming face.

"Oh. Hold on a second…" He concentrated a moment, magically clearing the long grass, cutting the bushes into neat hedges. Then he tossed the cube into the middle of the town lot.

It unfolded in mid-air, twisting and warping until the space was home to a large cloth pavilion with a hanging door flap beneath a canopy. The white canvas walls were delicately embroidered with flowers and vines which glinted in the afternoon light. Toggles held down window-flaps, short pieces of dowel stiffening their surrounds so they could be opened out.

Norman stepped forwards, pulling aside the door and hooking the flap up and out of the way.

"After you," he said, gesturing expansively.

Felicity stepped through the doorway hesitantly, uncertain, Peter following on her heels.

"Wow," he uttered looking around with wide eyes. "This is beautiful!"

Norman nodded. It was, indeed, beautiful; a fine entrance foyer carpeted with thick rugs over slate tiles. Far from the cloth walls that appeared to make up the outside, varnished wooden wall panels divided up the space, several rooms apparent. A spiral staircase leading to a second floor took up space in the centre of the room, and Peter ran off to explore the upstairs.

"This should be fully furnished, from what I can recall, with hot and cold water available in both the washroom and the kitchen. There's an automated privy, the lights are set to turn on and off with a clap," he clapped briefly to illustrate, "and there are multiple bedrooms. Gareth created a sunroom for you to work in—I believe that's it through the door to the left—it has a separate entrance so you can have a specific area for your shop.

"Like I said, the land is mine, so there's no rent. And the pavilion itself is secure. Nobody can enter without your knowledge. It doesn't look like much on the outside, but it's the finest mobile accommodation I've ever had the pleasure to see."

Felicity looked around with wide eyes. "This is all magic?" she asked. "I'm not certain…"

"It's not entirely magic. Especially now that it's been set up. Some of the comforts are driven by magical constructs, but they're fixed in place and will eventually run down without someone recharging them. You could do that yourself—you have the talent, and I could show you how to focus it."

Felicity shuddered and held herself. "No!" Then, softer, "No. I don't want to learn. I don't want to be a mage."

Norman shrugged. "Okay. So, do you want to live here? It will be cheaper. No more bills piling up from someone you don't like. And it will give you a bit of security for the next couple of months—Peter and I are going for a bit of a journey to meet some other mages."

Felicity nodded. "I suppose it's okay."

Peter came dashing down the stairs. "Mum, Mum, you have to see the bathtub…"

Chapter 16

653 OM Tarandeer

Year of the Leaping Rabbit

Bakar

Peter had never seen so many houses in one place. Suzie had drawn the wagon up the hill, and he could see Bakar stretched out below, filling the horizon, surrounded by flat fields of wheat.

"What do you think, boy?" Norman asked in that gravelled tone that he always used.

"It's so big! How do so many people exist? It must be the very centre of the Universe," he exclaimed, unable to conceive of anything larger.

Norman laughed, a big belly laugh that rumbled through his entire body.

"Bakar is just a town. A large town, to be sure, but just a town. Do you know, I've walked the halls of palaces that are bigger than Bakar?" Peter's eyes grew to saucers. "You'll get to see great cities and travel all of Varthien as a mage, boy. This is just your first step out of Pugton. Things will get exciting for you from here on out.

"See that, Suzie? Almost there and you can take a break. Are you okay to keep moving or do you need a top-up?"

Suzie's response was to simply start moving again, wending her way down the hill and along the road, towards the mass of civilization.

The town itself filled Peter's senses with the smell of hundreds of meals loaded with unfamiliar spices. The houses, many two or three storeys high, seemed to prop each other up, with no space between for garden plots, grass, trees. Instead, people hung pots from balcony railings, growing bright flowers or sparse vegetables in the tiny space sunlight touched. Pulleys connected ropes overhead from one side of the street to the other so clothes could hang in the breeze, and gutters directed water from the rooftops into buckets and barrels, presumably for drinking or bathing.

Peter's eyes snagged on each new innovation, hungry for the ways in which, implemented correctly, it could save him time at home.

The people mostly ignored the strange wagon. Children here or there stopped in their small groups to stare and point at Suzie, but among the adults they passed there was little to no reaction. As they moved slowly along the road, the throng became thicker, the road muddier, and the smells changed to ones less like food and more like sweat and offal. Obvious signs of permanent shops became more frequent, and Peter marvelled at the sheer number of services on offer.

"We'll be turning up ahead. Scaramond's. He's got a lad about your age that you're bound to get on with. We'll be staying for a number of days. Give you a bit of a chance to immerse yourself in another mage's style. Learn from others. That's the way we grow."

With a jolt, Suzie turned down the narrow alleyway and away from the crowd. The mud of the road firmed up, and in some places, Peter could see that there were actual cobblestones beneath the muck. Still, Suzie's feet were placed silently, with none of the racket of horses that had echoed through those more populous streets, and the only sound was the swish of the wheels on the road.

A slight tickle in the hair above Peter's ear reminded him that he had an extra passenger, and he reached up to check that the small dragon was secure.

"More mage," a tiny voice whispered, so soft that Peter barely heard it.

Norman looked across at him in response to the movement and noticed the dragon.

"Really? You brought the wyrm? She's not a pet, Peter. Don't treat her like one."

"She wanted to come," Peter pouted. "I told her we were going to see a city and she got excited."

Norman sighed. "Too late now, I suppose. Just keep her hidden so she doesn't get stolen. Dragons aren't common, and fetch a high price."

Peter was shocked at the idea of selling a creature like a dragon. It was like selling a baby! Carefully he flipped his shaggy hair over his ear so that the wyrm had greater cover.

"Hiding," the voice whispered, so soft that Peter was uncertain if he had actually heard a voice or just imagined it.

"Hiding," Peter echoed, and Norman looked at him sharply.

"Don't be obvious. No matter what." Then Norman turned back to watching the path before them, holding the ineffectual reins as if Suzie was a strange, grey horse.

Scaramond's tower was very different to Norman's. A large walled estate in West Bakar, the wide round tower surrounded by curated gardens and set upon a hill in the middle. Peter counted the windows in the side and was stunned to realise that there were at least 10 floors, possibly another beneath the pointed roof, and this tower might even have basements! A small stable stood beside the tower, convenient to the drive of gleaming crushed marble that approached the dark, heavyset door.

"Remember, address me as Master while we're here. Scaramond is a bit of a stickler for tradition," muttered Norman. Peter nodded slightly, watching carefully as a tall and slender man dressed in ornate, flowing red robes stepped out the door and waited patiently, clasping one hand in the other. He appeared youthful—perhaps in his early twenties—and clean-faced. Peter wondered how a mage this young managed to have an apprentice, but supposed that once out of apprenticeship, any mage could gain an apprentice of their own.

Scaramond remained there, unmoving, until Norman had finished unhitching the wagon and folding it, at which time he stepped forward. "Greetings, fellow mage. I offer you and your court sanctuary that you might find respite. Rest and be filled."

Norman bowed low. "My thanks, gracious host. I bear good will and respect. I and my court accept your offer in peace that we rest and be filled."

Norman straightened, holding out both hands. Scaramond stepped forward and took him into a hug.

Stepping back, Norman motioned to Peter. "This is my new apprentice, Peter. Only a couple of weeks since he took the brand, so this is the first time he's seen the ritual.

"Peter, what you just saw was a traditional pact. The mage whose land is being entered greets first. If it's a friendly interaction, there's an offer of sanctuary. The other mage thanks the host and accepts, stating that there is good will. The hug shows the host that the visitor isn't holding weapons, and reveals any body armour concealed under robes."

"What happens if they're not friendly?" Peter asked innocently.

Scaramond looked uncomfortable as Norman pursed his lips then turned the question around on Peter. "What do *you* think happens when people aren't friendly?"

Peter screwed up his face in thought. "I think maybe they tell them to go away, and if they don't, they start fighting."

"Got it in one, Peter. And it's not nice when mages fight each other, so we try not to do that very often."

Peter nodded.

"Precocious one on your hands then?" Scaramond muttered to Norman as they stepped through the massive oaken doors, "I don't let mine question me. Too much bother. He's got his tasks for the day laid out and I don't want to waste time answering silly questions."

"I'm raising Peter in much the same way as Albert raised me. His theory was that enquiring minds move fast and make breakthroughs we never consider. Perhaps he's right."

Scaramond turned to Peter. "What's your sense trigger boy?"

But Peter didn't even hear the question—he was engrossed in the sights around him. Rich red carpet with a deep pile covered the unwalled expanse of the lowest tower floor. Bookshelves covered the walls and could be seen lining the mezzanine second and third floors. Couched chairs and low tables were scattered around the room, each accompanied by a floating, overhead light that gleamed soft and yellow. A staircase graced the centre of the room, with polished wooden bannisters and stairs that seemed to rise of their own accord.

Occasional breaks in the bookshelves offered wall space that was covered by ornately framed pictures of people and places that Peter had only dreamed could exist. His eyes drifted to one—a ship on raging water—and he struggled to think it could be real. Surely that much water in one place was impossible.

Norman's bony finger poked him in the shoulder, releasing him from his visual journey.

"Our host asked you a question. Address him as Sir and respond."

"Oh, sorry Sir," he said. "What was the question again?"

"Sense trigger. What's yours?"

Peter looked at Norman wildly. "Nor... I mean Master, I don't know what that is!"

Norman was stumped. The boy had been displaying talents, how could he not know what his sense trigger was? "Just show us whatever it is you do to make the frogs ignore you."

"Okay," Peter said, then disappeared.

"Oh. Oh my. That's... that's... I don't know."

Norman was taken aback. The last time he had seen Peter playing in the marsh, he had still been visible. All he had known was that Peter had managed to hide his life-force. The invisibility was a new facet to the spell that was completely surprising.

"Reach out for him, Scaramond. See what he's doing in its entirety."

The thin man drew a pin from his lapel and lightly pricked the flesh between two of his fingers. His eyes changed colour until they looked like a frosted window on a winter's day, and he looked around. Five breaths passed, then ten, then fifteen, before he stopped turning and said, "I can't find him. Your resting gargoyle is there, but your apprentice is gone."

Peter reappeared, worried that there was something wrong with what he was doing. "I'm sorry, I didn't mean to. I'll stop and never do it again."

"No!" Norman thundered. "Never apologise. You're doing something right, boy. You're just doing it in a way we've never seen before." Then, quieter, he turned to his fellow mage. "What's your take?"

Scaramond took a long, deep breath, steepling his fingers before his lips. "Instantaneous. Not even a blink. No leakage. He reappeared and I could see his echo, but it hadn't been there even a second before." He rounded on the child. "Did you go somewhere different?"

"No, I didn't even move," wailed Peter, still worried that he was in trouble.

"He's a prodigy! Complete invisibility. Even if there's

leakage, I'm guessing it will only be when he's moving, and that will be miniscule—more from the movement of atoms around him.

"What else can you do, child?" Scaramond leant down so that he was face to face with the ten-year-old.

"I-I-I don't know, sir."

"Well then, we'll have to change that. Discipline. That's what you need. A disciplined mind can capture the secrets of the universe."

Sceptical, Norman's eyebrow raised, but he said nothing, just standing back and feeding Suzie some tailings out of his pocket as Scaramond called books to his hand with a pin pressed to his wrist, then handed the tall stack to Peter.

"Carry these, child. I'll show you to your chambers, then you can meet Chance in the study. Chance will show you his techniques, and we'll get you emulating some effects."

Peter wasn't quite sure what 'emulating' meant, but he nodded as he tried to keep all of the books balanced, then followed the two adult mages as they stepped onto the strangely moving staircase. It was an odd feeling to be rising in this way, and he wobbled, sure he would fall, until Norman's hand on his shoulder steadied him.

They rose and rose, winding past the three floors of bookshelves, up through a space in the ceiling into a lush garden filled with soft light, continuing up past wood-panelled hallways until they reached a circular room with doors all around and a large, glowing orb about the size of Peter's head floating in the centre.

"This is the guest chamber. Norman, I take it you'd like mountain views?" Norman nodded, and Scaramond turned to Peter. "What would you like to look out on from the windows? You can choose any sort of landscape—deserts, jungles, battlefields even, if that's to your liking."

Peter thought for only a second before he said, carefully, "Is the picture downstairs of the boat on lots of water the sort of place you can show me? I've never seen something like that before. It looks like the water goes forever. I like that."

Scaramond blinked, then said, "Oh, the ocean scene? Certainly." He placed a hand onto the orb, and pointed them each to different doorways, now with glowing lanterns over the lintel.

Peter stepped through his doorway, into a large, carpeted suite with an enormous bed, dressers, a low circular table with two plush chairs. A panelled door stood on the left, but what took up Peter's sight was the wall of glass directly before him, which looked out upon a vast ocean. The susurration of the constantly moving water played gently in his ears, and a distinct but pleasant smell of salt water filled his nostrils. A small balcony was visible beyond the glass wall, and Peter surmised that there must be a doorway leading onto that tiny landing, but before he could step further into the room, Scaramond started speaking, laying a surprisingly heavy hand on his shoulder to hold him back from exploring.

"Through the doorway you will find bathing and ablution facilities. The two buttons on the bath are for hot and cold water, red and blue for the respective temperatures. The yellow button next to the privy will remove all waste. And the white button on the wall will send a blast of warm air to dry you after washing," Scaramond intoned in a bored voice. "The study is on the next floor up. Come, don't dawdle."

The three once again stepped onto the rising stairway, which took them to the next floor, a brightly lit expanse with dozens of tables lined with uncomfortable looking chairs. A couple of tables held piles of books stacked neatly, but most were clean and bare. Peter gratefully put the books he was carrying down onto the nearest table.

A small figure with an open book sat at one of the desks, but Peter couldn't quite see them behind the tall stack of books they were obviously studying from.

"Here you will spend most of your time. You will work side-by-side with my apprentice, Chance. Chance's sense trigger is voice. I expect it will complement your… um… whatever it is you use. You and Chance can work to the same schedule.

"Chance, come meet your new study partner."

A small, weedy looking boy stepped out from behind the pile of books. A mop of dirty blond hair fell into the brown eyes of the very pale, very young face. It looked like Chance never went outside, thought Peter. The boy wore flowing blue robes of something that looked much finer than the homespun linen tunic and pants that Peter was accustomed to, but the long sleeves that fell over the back of the boy's hands looked unsuitable for a lot of the daily tasks that Peter took for granted. The boy stepped forward to stand by Scaramond's side, then in a very soft voice, almost a whisper, said, "Pleased to meet you." Tucking both hands together into his sleeves, he bowed to Peter very slightly, then turned back to his master. Scaramond nodded to him, and Chance returned to his books.

Norman spoke up for the first time since they had stood on the bottom floor. "The reason you are here, Peter, is to learn how other mages apply their power. You will have years to learn how I do things, but that may not always be appropriate to your studies. Master Scaramond has the largest collection of literature written about magical effects in Varthien. We are incredibly fortunate that he lives so close to us. For the next two weeks, you will study as many books as you can, following the same regimen as Chance here so that Chance may guide you. Do everything that Master Scaramond tells you to do.

"Judging by the books you've been carrying, your first task will be looking at water magic. This is a fairly simple magic and should take you no time to master. Read up about it here, but don't try to apply it unless you're on the testing floor, which I believe is the next floor up…"

Norman looked across at the other mage to confirm his belief, and was granted a nod.

"Yes, the next floor up. If you need me at all, you'll likely find me in the garden, though I may join you in here from time to time. We're never too old to learn, and I am here to learn just as you are."

Peter nodded and wiped his hair out of his eyes. Scaramond, catching the movement, also spotted something else.

"What's this? Another addition to your entourage, Norman? Is that a wyrmling?" he asked, his eyes gleaming with curiosity and another emotion Peter couldn't quite recognise.

Norman nodded. "I told Peter not to bring it, but he's wilful. Peter seems to be treating it like a pet, which goes against the grain, but it's his responsibility and if the wyrmling tolerates it, so be it."

Scaramond bowed deeply towards Peter, addressing the wyrm, "I am humbled to be in such esteemed company. If I had been aware, I would have prepared suitable lodgings for you beforehand. You are welcome to this home for as long as I remain, and I shall ever be your most humble servant. When we break to dine, I shall have a place created for you where you may rest in comfort."

The tiny voice, so soft it might not even exist, said, "Thank you."

Peter, surmising that he was the only one who had heard it, spoke up. "She says 'thank you', sir."

Norman's surprise washed visibly over his face. "She's speaking?"

"Yes, Master. She doesn't talk much, and her voice is as small as she is so she's really hard to hear, but she talks to me."

"She?" Scaramond asked. "She sparks? I know a most appropriate gift in that case. And now I must get back to my duties. I will see you all in the dining hall at 6:00 sharp." With that, he turned and ascended the staircase.

Norman shortly made his way downstairs, leaving Peter and the wyrm with the silent Chance.

It turned out that Chance wasn't just silent out of respect or fear of his elders, Peter discovered as he tried to strike the boy up in conversation. Each time Peter asked a question, Chance would respond by scribbling a brief answer in a notepad he kept to one side. The hand was fluid, neat and practiced, Peter saw, far different from his own untidy scrawl. Soon, he had discerned why, as Chance wrote, "My trigger is my voice. I cannot speak openly to you in case I accidentally set off magical effects."

Peter sighed, disappointed that there would be no speech between them, but then brightened when he realized they could have secret written conversations when the adults were in the room. Together, they made plans to pass notes when they wanted to converse, and friendship started to form.

The books were dry and boring. There were stories about the sorts of water effects that had been shown through the centuries — making it rain, filling a cup with water, bringing forth water from the ground, creating creatures made of water to fight in wars, even nasty effects like encasing people in bubbles of water so that they would drown on solid land. The stories went on, discussing the sort of sense triggers that had been used to make these effects. Some sense triggers seemed simple, like the mage who could summon effects by clicking his tongue a certain way, whereas others seemed more complex, like the mage who needed to draw a large circle filled with strange glyphs written in a language only he knew. One mage had covered his body in tattoos so that he could easily touch an image associated with the effect he wanted. Another carried different fruits and herbs because his sense trigger was taste.

And yet, none of these seemed to be anything like what he had done to keep the frogs from noticing him. Then, he had simply wanted to be quiet. The more he practiced, the quieter he got, so that now he could pick the alarm frogs up and they would barely even notice.

By the time dinner had rolled around, he was frustrated and confused.

Dinner on the fifth floor was a grand affair. The wood-panelled walls were warm and inviting, the deep blue carpet softened all footsteps, and stepping through the doors at the end of the hall opened up to a long table covered in food. Long drapes were open to show the sun setting over Bakar, and from this height the town seemed to reach all the way to the horizon.

Places had been set for all six tower occupants — Suzie and the young wyrm included, and appropriate meals floated to each place setting. Suzie's plate was covered in a strange assortment of twigs, ribbons, and greasy pastes, but she seemed to enjoy herself, licking the plate clean with noisy stone-on-ceramic clinks. The wyrmling was offered tiny piles of metallic dusts, which she appeared to vacuum into her petite body. Peter was half-convinced he could see her growing as she ate the rich meal, but he shook this off, thinking that this was merely his imagination.

The rest of them, all human, ate roast meats and vegetables, glistening with fats and gravy, followed by fruit pies smothered in sweet, yellow custard, until they were all replete.

Peter sat back in his chair, feeling so stuffed that he could barely move.

Scaramond rose from his chair and knelt by the tiny wyrmling. "As promised, I have a gift for you." He reached into a pocket and drew out a small bottle filled with oil. A whitish-silver lump sat in the bottom of the jar.

"Some metals are quite hard to come across in nature," he said in a reverent voice, "and are volatile to handle. This is a lump of pure sodium. It will burn when exposed to air. I don't know exactly what its effects will be on your constitution, but I have read that some draconids prize sodium-rich meals. I offer this in hope of a friendship that lasts far into the future."

The wyrmling had risen up to show attentiveness to Scaramond's words, the very topmost point of its 10cm length (which Peter assumed to be her head) nodding and moving in response. When he put the thimble-sized jar onto the table and pulled out the cork, the wyrmling immediately jumped in, ducking deep into the oil to reach the white metal chunk at the bottom. The mage had come prepared, offering her a soft cloth to dry on as she clambered out, then, dry, she moved to a clear spot on the table and let out a stream of yellow fire, twice as long as her body and almost too bright to look at. Nodding curtly to the group, she turned and made a deep bow to Scaramond.

The mage smiled and capped the tiny jar. To Peter's eyes, the lump of metal remained unchanged, but perhaps that was because her jaws were so small, he thought to himself. The new metal had obviously had an effect, though — just yesterday her spark had looked simply like a flint-and-steel strike.

Bedtime held yet another surprise. The wyrm had returned to her place behind Peter's ear as they all ascended to the guest quarters, and she asked him, "Petunia?"

Peter's eyes opened wide, realising he had forgotten a very important thing — the wyrmling's bed.

"Oh! Petunia!"

Scaramond turned, a quizzical look on his face. "Petunia?" he asked.

"Just the wyrm..." Peter began, but wasn't able to finish before Scaramond's reaction.

"I am pleased to finally have your name, Mistress Petunia."

"Oh, that's not her name," Peter stuttered, but was interrupted by the tiny voice in his ear.

"Good name. I like."

"… It appears I am wrong," he amended. "That is now her name. But I was referring to Petunia's bed, which is a potted petunia plant that she sleeps in."

"She sleeps in a flower?"

"No. In the soil at the base of the flower..."

"You relegate this magnificent creature to sleep in the dirt like a commoner?" Scaramond's face took on rage and thunder, directed soundly at Peter, until Norman put a hand on the other mage's shoulder.

"The wyrmling—Petunia—sleeps on her hoard. As her hoard is in the pot, and it is too heavy for her to relocate, the petunia is her bed."

Scaramond grunted in displeasure. Directing his attention at the tiny dragon, he pointed towards Peter's room. "I have arranged for your slumber, Milady. You will find a silver orb upon the dresser. It houses a door of suitable size for your free entry and departure. In lieu of your hoard, you shall find within a bed of eider, silk, and cloth of gold for you to rest upon."

Norman frowned a little at the extravagance being thrust upon the wyrmling, but remained silent until the mage stopped speaking.

"Ahem. Well, the day has been long and we must get an early start tomorrow. Thank you for your diligence in providing us hospitality. We shall now retire."

Scaramond nodded, then headed upstairs as Norman remained still, his hand holding Peter back from the room awaiting him. Once the mage was out of sight and earshot, Norman spoke up, addressing Petunia.

"He offers you much, and you are very young, so it may not be obvious yet, but generally when someone gives you something there is an expectation that they will get something in return. Perhaps it's not immediate, but sooner or later they will call the favour in. And the larger the gift that has been offered, the larger the implicit obligation. Be wary. It's okay to take Master Scaramond's gifts, but it may mean that you'll need to do something large in return for him someday.

"Now go, both of you. Rest. We have much work tomorrow." He turned to his quarters, laying a brief, familiar hand on Suzie's shoulder as he passed her still form before disappearing through the door.

Following breakfast the next day, they headed to the test

floor rather than to the study.

This floor was bare stone, floor and ceiling both, ringed with unglazed, open-arched windows. The stairway, which had been magical up to this point, ended, and a manual stair took its place.

"This floor has no magics that could interfere with your casting," Scaramond said to Peter. "The idea is to give you a completely clean environment to experiment in. How did your studies go yesterday?"

Peter shrugged his shoulders, scratched is head, and scrunched up his nose. "I guess I just don't get it. Everybody talks about doing a bunch of stuff, and I tried to think of what I do, and it just doesn't seem like it works like my stuff."

Norman knelt down on one knee and looked directly into Peter's eyes. "You just think about what you want to happen when you turn invisible, right?" Peter nodded. "So how about you do what you do for turning invisible, but at the same time think about doing something you read about yesterday?"

"Okay," Peter said, then turned invisible.

Scaramond had been watching intently with frosted blue eyes, a pin pressed to the flesh between two of his fingers. "You can stop now, Peter. Come back."

Peter reappeared with a jolt.

"Hmm. Interesting. Norman, I need you to watch the play of energy as Peter does that again, and tell me if you see the same thing I do.

"Peter, I need you to turn invisible, then go as quickly as you can around the outside of the room—run if you're able—then come back to this spot and reappear."

With both mages watching, Peter disappeared.

Norman and Scaramond struggled to see the faintest trace of energy as Peter ran around the room, then watched as he reappeared before them.

Norman jerked in surprise. "That's impossible!"

Scaramond looked at Peter with eyes that had returned to

their former green. "How do you feel, child?" he asked.

"Cold, sir."

Indeed, Peter was shivering, his teeth chattering slightly.

"Do you always feel cold after being invisible?"

"Yes, sir. It's worse now that I've been running, though."

The mages looked at each other. "He's not expending magic, he's conserving it. Stockpiling it." Norman said.

"That's what I saw too. His reservoir is larger now than it was when he started. I think he's actually stealing the kinetic energy of the atoms around him, turning it directly into potential energy inside himself."

"That could be a problem," Norman mused. "How about we discuss this elsewhere." He turned his attention to the boy.

"Peter, I'm going to free up your morning for you to explore Bakar." He pulled a small leather pouch from his robes. "Here is some spare coin for you to buy trinkets. You'll also find a doorknob in there in case you get lost. Just hold it against any wall and turn the handle and you will reappear in my chambers. However, I expect you not to use it; I expect you to find your way home *without* the use of magic.

"When you return this afternoon, I want you to start reading up on some other types of magic. I'll compile a list of books for you to read."

With that, Peter was dismissed, with Chance following after about a minute later. Together they collected Petunia and raced out the front doors, Peter desperate for sunshine and freedom.

Chapter 17

SUCCESSION

---

661 OM Tarandeer
Year of the Tangled Briar

Atinien Mountain

Not a trickle, but a flood. Mages had appeared from all corners of Varthien, and each was directed to the lodge outside, some muttering about leaving apprentices at home to wreck their experiments, many muttering about the cold, even more muttering about the state of lodging. However, each was able to find space in the seemingly small lodge house, its dimensionally altered halls offering thousands of rooms, each containing the basic necessities for a few nights' stay.

Norman set up the outdoor cooking facilities that had gone disused for most of his apprenticeship (and apparently had not been used since). Bonfires ringed the gathering space, and in the centre, a large cauldron of water bubbled and boiled on a smaller fire. Each mage, on arrival, was asked for their contribution to the pot, which seemed to never overflow and could contain far more than an ordinary pot. Some mages, showing extravagance, submitted entire carcasses; others offered herbs and spices. Norman saw one woman add a barrel of wine, barrel included. Not to worry, though. This cauldron sorted it all like some magical chef, offering up Miracle Stew — uniquely suited meals to every person who dipped a ladle.

Lines for the cauldron were long, both to give and receive, but the mages treated this time as a chance to strut, showing off their benevolence and abilities to their fellows in an attempt to raise their political stature. Elderly mages, far past the age of admittance to the council, jockeyed for favour with their younger counterparts, brokering for advisory positions or offering varied services. Small groups broke away from the strangely festive crowd to show each other newly developed applications of power, trading magical displays in an attempt to learn new techniques.

A knot of people gathered around the entrance to the cave system, and people lined the walls of Albert's private abode, breaking the peaceful atmosphere with debates and raucous conversation. Norman had installed the succession box outside the entrance immediately after releasing the call and each mage of age was offered a chance to submit their touch for admission to the council.

A hulking man dressed in bright yellow silks explained to Norman that each touch would be weighed by the universe for aptitude, skill, along with several personality traits that had been allocated several thousand years ago in the time of OM Barduce. Additionally, each Highmage was able to suggest one name, which would then be given a small weight to raise its ranking. Once the submission time had expired, a list of the top five ranked names would be produced. The top name would be the top candidate, but only if they were socially acceptable. After all, it wouldn't do for a choice picked by the box to cause civil unrest, thus the option of runners up.

After selection, all council members would gather together so Albert could name who among them would be the new Magus. It was the right of a Magus to name his successor from the twelve Highmages. If he passed away before naming a new Magus, the 12 names would be placed inside the box for the selection to be made by the supposedly unbiased universe. It was not unknown for factions to develop to place pressure onto an elderly Magus to name their preferred candidate, but supposedly the succession box reduced the likelihood of the leader's premature demise.

Within two hours, the mass of people was oppressive. Each time Norman stepped outside, he felt overwhelmed by the sheer size of the crowd, and distressed at the jovial atmosphere that many mages seemed to be displaying. How many of these people had ever met Albert, he wondered. How many even realized that what they were celebrating was the imminent death of a kind, generous person? Each happy yell of recognition as friends encountered each other after long periods of separation cut into him until his grief became a ball of hot anguish inside his chest. Head down, he avoided conversations in the fear that he would explode in a torrent of invective, confining his responses to "Sorry, can't talk…"

Every few minutes, he would be greeted with a new task, always deemed by the demanding supplicant to be 'urgent'. He dashed from each request to the next, default dogsbody to a crowd of thousands.

Seeing Norman's harried expression, a red-robed mage caught his arm as he carted buckets of water and bundles of cloth to the over-subscribed outhouse.

"You don't need to be doing all this, Norman. It's too much with all that's happening. I'll get a work team together — we have enough old coots out there with nothing better to do than strut. I'm sure we have plenty to take over the nitty-gritty. You just see to Albert. He needs you more than we do right now."

Norman nodded, vaguely registering that the voice belonged to Scaramond. The bucket and towels were gently removed from his arms and he blindly turned back to the door set into the rocky face of the mountain.

True to his words, Scaramond took less than 10 minutes to establish a presence at the doorway to Albert's bedroom, and only five more to eject all the interlopers from the halls. As the buzz of conversation died down, Norman was once more able to breathe, and peace reigned again. He took up the chair by Albert's bed and kept vigil. Occasionally he would hear the low muttering of someone seeking his attention, but obviously these queries were all redirected to whichever member of Scaramond's team was deemed most appropriate, as nobody was granted entry.

Nearing mealtime, he stepped up from the chair by Albert's bed to prepare a meal, but was stopped at the doorway by an unfamiliar man. "Can Albert leave his bed briefly? We have a sedan chair awaiting him and would like to give him a meal at the lodge and an opportunity to speak to the candidates.

Albert was awake, his eyes twinkling in the dim light of the room. "I think I can manage a short outing, don't you, boy?" he said, more of a statement than a question. "Give the crowd a little looksie. There's no need for you to be cooking when we've got a feast next door. Can't be rude and turn down a dinner invitation, can we? Especially at the event of the decade — nay, the century."

With the assistance of an arm each side, Albert huffed his way to the doorway and into the sedan chair. The two volunteers took their places fore and aft, gently lifted the chair, and carried it outside, with Norman bringing up the rear.

Someone had been prepared for this brief journey. A sturdy roll of carpet had been laid across the slush, reaching from the mountain entrance to the lodge. Someone must have tempered the crowd's mood, as there was no revelry amongst the crowd that lined each side of the carpet, paying homage to the man who had directed the Council's movements for more than 660 years.

There was a brief stop at the stew pot for Albert to touch the handle of the ladle, and an aide filled a plate for him, carrying it ahead of the slower sedan chair so that it could be there for Albert when he arrived. Norman, too, was ushered to the pot by an unhurried Scaramond, appearing as calm as he had been earlier.

"Perks of being the caregiver," the mage whispered in his ear. "You should not be waiting in lines on a day like this."

Albert was seated at the centre of the head table, six council members either side of him. Norman was seated on the nearest table, Scaramond ousting a puffed-up Delingaard mage wearing bright pink silks covered in brass sequins who was sitting in the seat closest to the end. The man's loud objections were quickly stifled with a sharp, muttered conversation, and with anger-filled backward looks, he was shuffled to a table further back in the expansive room.

Everyone ate, the clinks of cutlery against crockery the overwhelming sound, with a background murmur of conversation quietly filling the space. After some time, the council member in yellow silks that sat directly to the right of Albert stood, clinking a spoon against the fine crystal wine glass in his hand. The ringing sound quieted the chatter, and he began to speak.

"For those who don't know me, I am Bellamy Foljur, current oldest council member. We have all been gathered here today for a very serious purpose. Magus Albert Tarandeer has chosen to leave us, and has offered us the opportunity to determine a successor before his death."

The background murmur became louder for a moment, then settled as Bellamy raised both his hands.

"Succession was once a difficult matter. Those of us who have been students of history may know the story I am about to tell, but for some of you this will be a new story.

"5750 years ago, the brief dynasty of Our Magus Fellin occurred. It was expected that Our Magus Fellin would hold the reins of office for centuries, but he fell from a horse just 24 years into his stewardship.

"Nobody was prepared for this. It was a time of great change in Varthien, and political powers wished to take charge of the Council of Mages. Factions arose, demanding this person or the next person take charge, but the volatility of the situation meant that when any single mage appeared to gain favour, something would happen to hinder that progress, and usually, that something was death.

"The Highmage War lasted four years and resulted in the death of thousands of mages. Few survivors remained. Of those survivors, Our Magus Barduce was instated to lead the council. And in year four of Our Magus Barduce's reign, eight years after the death of Our Magus Fellin, he created the succession box, which he used to stabilise the still fluctuating council.

"This box is our answer to the Highmage War. Never again shall we have uncertainty over succession, as the Universe is given the choice. This is a choice free of political sway and cultural bias. Every mage of age who places a hand upon this box is given a chance to join the council as a Highmage, weighted by instructions inside the box that can only be altered by the sitting Magus.

"If you are 70 years or younger and have not yet touched the box, I encourage you to do so this evening. The nominations process only lasts 24 hours, so by midmorning tomorrow we will know who our new Highmage is.

"As we are seeing out a Magus, though, he will then be able to determine his successor from the 13 Highmage candidates. That timeframe will be determined by Our Magus Albert Tarandeer, who is seated to my left tonight."

With that, he sat.

Albert looked around, then shouted, "Where's my boy?"

Norman jumped up immediately and came around to Albert, who asked for assistance to stand.

"Ah, my apprentice, Norman, everybody. Best apprentice I ever had.

"I just wanted to tell all you youngsters out there that living for a long time isn't everything people think it is. We can live as long as we want, you know. There are people in this room who are so old I don't understand how they can stand it. If you get to a point where you are extending your life just so you can find new ways to extend your life, you're doing it wrong. Best to bow out when I'm still able to connect to the world than to forget what that connection is like and live on far past my usefulness.

"Keep striving. Keep doing your best for the others around you. Make the world a better place."

He slumped into Norman's arms. "Take me back to my bed now, boy. I need to sleep."

As the sedan chair lifted Magus Albert Tarandeer and filed out of the dining hall, every mage in the room stood and bowed low to the elderly man.

Chapter 18

661 OM Tarandeer
Year of the Tangled Briar

Pugton

Reginald planted his hand firmly against the white stucco and leant his weight on that one straight arm. He angled his torso in, breathing ale-scented breath on the face of the girl before him.

Her wide eyes looked around for an escape from his attentions.

"Reggie, stop, please. I need to get to me mam's with this stuff. I'll be in dreadful shite if I take too long." She moved the basket further in front of her, between her slender body and his larger, pudgy form.

"We're not doing nothing," he said. "You can tell the old coot off. I just want to talk to you is all." His spare hand reached out to grasp a stray lock of her long, dark hair, stroking the side of her face as he did.

"No, Reggie. I said no." She pushed her basket more firmly against his torso, trying to get a little space. He shifted slightly, and she ducked under his arm, hurrying quickly away from him so she couldn't be trapped against the wall again. "I said I have to go."

"I just wanted to talk," he yelled at her fleeing back, then after a moment of muddled thought, unsteadily started to wander back to the tavern.

"She was beggin' for it. Beggin'." he muttered to anyone in earshot, which mostly just included himself. "Doesn't know what she passed up on…"

He stepped aside to allow a cart to pass by, then turned, staring at the oddity. That wasn't a short, grey horse pulling that cart, he realised slowly. It was a big cat. It looked like it had some sort of rough, greyish-brown hide, or maybe was something covered in cloth that had been dipped in mud.

"What're you… Oi! Stop! What're you doing?" he yelled out at the person sitting in the odd cart. "What're you doing bringing this…" he searched for a word, "…dangerous creature into my town? What is it, anyway? It looks weird. Get out!"

Peter looked at the obviously drunk, very rotund teenager as Suzie stepped off the side of the road to park the wagon. The puffing, red face was familiar, so he stepped down and approached his former tormentor.

"Reginald, isn't it?" Peter asked, knowing full well that it definitely was.

Reginald looked up at Peter. Where, just eight years ago, Reginald had been the taller lad, Peter was now head and shoulders above him. And, far from the healthy muscle Peter had built up from daily woodcutting, water carrying, and tower maintenance, Reginald was soft. Flabby.

"Whoa, you're a big one," Reginald drawled, taking an exaggerated step back. "Anyway, you can't bring that… thing…" he waggled a finger in Suzie's general direction, "into Pugton. It's against rules."

Peter's eyes opened in mock surprise. "Oh! I didn't know. I guess I should see the rules to make certain I'm not breaking any more of them."

"Well," blustered Reginald, "I don't know where… Um, I'm not sure where the rules are listed. You'll have to talk to the mayor. Or someone. But we've never had a thing like that..." the finger started waggling wildly at Suzie again, "...in this town before and it's definitely against rules."

Peter frowned severely but spoke in an even tone. "I don't think I ever heard of these rules before. They must be new. After all, that 'thing'..." he waggled his finger in a mockery of Reginald's wild gesticulation, "... is here quite often—at least once a month—and this has never been mentioned. But I will, indeed, talk to the mayor—I presume Calder Wainwright is still in the position—and get an update. It wouldn't do for people to be misinformed about these things. I'll be certain to let him know that Reginald Cutler is diligent about policing these requirements."

Reginald's face went splotchy—red in places, white in others, and he was sweating quite heavily. His voice rose both in pitch and volume.

"Look, Mr Wainwright is a busy man, so no need to bother him. Just take your cat-thing and go. We don't like strangers."

"You don't remember me, do you?" Peter asked, speaking in a low, calm voice. "I was born in this town. My mother lives just a few streets away from here. So not a stranger. Not even close to being a stranger.

"I remember you though. How could you have changed so little from when we were kids? You were a bully then, and you're obviously still that bully."

Reginald was breathing quite heavily now, huffing and puffing through his nose, his mouth a thin, twitchy line that looked like it was trying to disappear.

"You... you... I don't... you..."

Obviously lacking the ability to form a comeback, he turned sharply and walked away, his hands fists held stiffly to his sides.

Petunia popped her head out of Peter's pocket.

"That was him," she said, fearfully.

"Who, Reginald? That's the mean boy you say stole your

coin?"

Petunia nodded, extricating herself from the cloth and flying up to look Peter in the eyes. "Yes. The mean boy. He's a thief, and he's a murderer, and he's mean, and he's a thief."

Petunia grew agitated, flying around in a dizzying feat of choreography. "He's a mean boy and a thief. And he murders."

"You said that. A couple of times now. What do you mean, he murders? You didn't tell me that earlier," Peter asked, worried.

"He killed all my brothers. And all my sisters. And all the ones who didn't know yet if they were brothers or sisters. And he chopped them all up and he fed them to fishes and he cut out my mother's tongue and he tied her down and everybody died."

Peter tried to make sense of the story, but he had difficulty following Petunia's logic.

"Reginald did all this?"

Petunia nodded.

"He did all of this while he was stealing your coin last night?"

"No, he did it all when I was little. I'm big now."

"He stole your coin when you were little?"

"No, he stole my coin last night. He killed everyone when I was little. We need to get him. We need to make him tell us where my coin is."

Less certain now than he had been when they set out this morning, Peter started walking toward the butcher's shop.

Chapter 19

653 OM Tarandeer
Year of the Leaping Rabbit

Bakar

The two boys explored the markets with glee, playing hide and seek with each other amongst the colourful tents and displays. Occasionally, Peter would stop to stare at products, thinking how his mother would love the bright silk threads and fabrics on display.

Intent now on buying a gift, Peter crossed the way to an open silversmith while Chance was distracted by the range at a travelling bookseller. The freshly wrought needles and glass-headed pins glistened in the morning sunlight. Looking up to speak to the jeweller, his eye was caught by a trove of colourful marbles.

Marbles! With a morning to spare and a new friend, what better than to play? With a broad smile, he handed over a couple of heavy coins and received a small pouch with ten pieces of round glass clicking together, three silver needles, a long, sharp hatpin, and a few scraps of wire so short that the smith was happy to pass them across to the earnest child. Then, with a whoop and a holler, Peter pulled the silent Chance away from the books and down the road towards a green park, stopping only to pick up some honey-cakes.

Peter divided the marbles up and, with a circle traced in the dirt, they smacked each other's colourful spheres out of the ring. They played tag and ran around. They climbed trees. And occasionally, the games and fun would make Chance laugh, iridescent bubbles appearing around the boy at each vocalisation. Each time this happened, the boy clapped both hands over his mouth, a scared look on his face.

"Why are you scared?" Peter asked. "There's nothing wrong with bubbles! Look!"

He reached out a finger, expecting it to pop like a soap bubble. Instead, it clung to his finger, decreasing quickly in size until it had disappeared completely, as if sucked into the skin.

Chance frowned, reaching out to try the same thing, but the bubble popped, much in the same way that Peter had expected the first bubble to.

"That's so weird!" Peter said, and ran about trying it again and again. Each time, the bubble clung to Peter's skin, drawing itself in. After a half-dozen bubbles, Peter's finger started to tingle and twitch, as if it was full of energy.

Concerned, Chance tugged on Peter's sleeve. *We need to go back*, he wrote on his notepad. *Masters need to know about this.*

Peter pouted, but nodded, and together they walked back to the tower, Peter dragging his feet and Chance dragging Peter.

Norman and Scaramond were deep in conversation when the boys returned, earlier than either man had anticipated. Their conversation halted abruptly as Chance sat down heavily on the seat next to them and started scribbling away frantically.

Peter does strange things with my accidental bubbles, he wrote cryptically. *We need to show you on the test floor. Come see!*

"Accidental bubbles?" asked Norman. "I don't understand." But he dutifully followed the boys, Scaramond taking up the rear.

Tickle me, the paper that Chance shoved into Peter's hand read. Shrugging his shoulders, he did as he was told, and soon Chance's laughter filled the floor with big, floating bubbles.

Chance poked a couple with a finger, showing the adults how easily they popped. Then he elbowed his companion.

"Oh, right, yeah," said Peter, uncomfortable with the attention. He found the largest bubble and stabbed at it with his hand, coming into contact with a few more on the way. As before, the bubbles clung to him, sucking into his skin.

"Stop immediately," snapped Norman, alarmed. "Sorry, I'm not angry, just concerned. Scaramond and I have already been discussing what's happening here." He looked across at the other man, resignation on his face.

"Peter, you seem to be storing up magical potential. Imagine everyone has a jug inside of them that they can fill with magic, which then can be used. Some people have smaller jugs than others." He pulled a milk jug out of one of his pockets to illustrate, strangely full of milk. "Say this jug is my store of magic, and I can use it for whatever I want to do."

The boys nodded, Peter wondering how Norman had managed to hold a jug of milk in his pocket without spilling it.

"Peter, you don't have a jug," Norman stated flatly. "Instead, you have this entire tower. When you only have this much milk—I mean magic—it's harder to use." Norman upended the milk jug on the floor and pointed down at the spill. "Try pouring that onto your cereal in the morning. You're not going to have any luck.

"What this means is that you're storing all of the spare magic around you. Until you've got a stockpile of energy, you'll have difficulty with release or control.

"We're going to give you a number of books to study over the next several days that will be about building your potential. A lot of these books are about mages that have exhausted themselves in big works and how they recovered, but you'll be using this as a starting point. You just need to learn not to steal it from other magic workings around you, because that won't win you friends in the wizarding community."

Nodding slowly, Peter considered what had just been said. "If I've got so much space to store up energy, how long will it be before I can use it?" he asked.

Scaramond lay a hand on his shoulder and stooped down to speak to him face-to-face. "Your magic will come when you are ready, and not before. That's okay. Some mages never have more than small talents, only available in their most trying moments. That's okay too. They are no less mages for that.

"You are able to do something most of us can't. You can turn your energy generation into an effect all of its own. Not only that, you can do it without relying on something exterior to you. You are a mage, and you are remarkable."

Peter felt his ears get hot and his face get prickly from the blush that spread across his skin. "Thank you, sir." Then, with gratitude, he put his hand into his pocket, tracing the shapes of a gift with his thumb. "I got you something…"

A small flick on his ear reminded him that he needed to attribute all sources of inspiration. "Um, Petunia and I got you something," he amended. "She suggested it and I bought it."

Clutched in his hand, he drew out the ornate hatpin. A silver triskelion seemed to gather the light and focus it toward a large yellow cabochon of glass in the centre of the head. His fingers stroked the smooth metal of the pin, feeling the tip to make certain there were no burrs.

"You've been so nice to Petunia, and we wanted to get you something nice in return.

"Mum's always losing her needles and pins. They fall on the floor and then it takes a long time to find them, and sometimes you find them by standing on them or sitting on them, and that must be really difficult for you because you use pins in your magic. So, I…we… got you this hatpin. It will look nice if you use it like a brooch, and the yellow will look good on your red clothing."

Peter held it out shyly, and Scaramond reverently took it in both hands. He studied the hatpin, his eyes growing frosty for a moment, so quickly that Peter barely caught the change, then a large smile grew over his face.

"This is truly a kingly gift, and I will treasure it," he said. "You are right, I do sometimes lose my sharps, and accidental injuries can set off unfortunate effects."

He removed the tiny, glass-headed pin from his lapel and proudly replaced it with the new, much longer and fancier, hatpin. Just as predicted, the clear, yellow glass looked like it was made specifically to be backed by the red robes the man wore.

"I will never need another pin. Thank you, both of you, for considering me.

"Now I go to gather books. There will be little time for anything other than study for you the rest of your time here, so I suggest you clean up and make the most of what morning you have left.

"And don't worry about your magic. I think you'll find it will come to you sooner than you think."

Chapter 20

661 OM Tarandeer
Year of the Tangled Briar

Pugton

It was Petunia who noticed her first.

As Peter focussed on the way ahead, looking for the place Reginald had retreated to, Petunia was free to look about, her new perch on Peter's shoulder offering a clear vantage. The ample form stood down a side-street, back to them but in obvious distress. Voluminous, multi-layered skirts, tight bodice, and fluffy sleeves, all printed with large pink roses, were topped with tightly curled hair under a frilled bonnet, but Petunia still recognised her.

Felicity was hopping from foot to foot, wringing her hands and casting anxious looks toward the large pavilion she had called her home for eight years.

"Peter, it's your mother," Petunia whispered into his ear.

"My mother? Make up your mind. First it was Reginald, now it's my mother? Do you even know who took your coin?"

"No, Peter," Petunia said, louder, tugging on his earlobe. "Look! Your mother!"

Turning his head, Peter saw that it was indeed his mother, albeit somewhat more plump than last time he had seen her.

"You're looking fancy, Mum, going somewhere special?" he asked.

Felicity visibly jumped, obviously not expecting a sound from behind her.

"Oh, Peter!" she said breathlessly, "You scared me! No, no, I'm not going anywhere special. This old thing is for around the house."

"Sorry for the fright, we were just in town and I saw you. We decided to say hello." Pointing at her hands, he asked, "Something wrong?"

Eying Suzie, and with frequent glances over her shoulder, her response seemed at odds with her demeanour. "I'm fine, just fine. You must be excited, eh? Freedom in—what is it—a week?"

Peter smiled. "Two days, Mum. The day after tomorrow. But I'm not really sure what I'm going to do with myself. Probably come home and loaf around for a little while, I suppose. Spend some time with you."

"Sounds good," Felicity mumbled, still distracted and looking frequently in the direction of the pavilion.

"Are you sure you're okay, Mum? You seem nervous. Something in the house?"

"Oh, I'm fine," she said, waving her hand nonchalantly. "It's just—there's a magic thing in there and I don't want to…"

"A magic thing? Isn't the house basically *made* of magic?"

"Not really, but…well, yes, I suppose. This is a different thing. Not part of the house. A new thing. And," she lowered her voice, "It's calling me *a mage*."

"Mum, you *are* a mage. You might not use magic often, but someone once told me that it's not a matter of using it or not. Anyone with magic potential is a mage."

"But I'm not… I don't want to be a mage." Felicity sighed. "How about I just show you?"

The doorway sizzled slightly as Peter approached it. Its edges glowed brightly, and tiny specks of golden light occasionally broke the scene that played out on the other side.

There, through the doorway, a bustling group of people — mages, Peter assumed from the vast array of robes visible in the crowd — walked hither and thither. Most seemed to be walking into or out of a small wooden lodge in the foreground. The background was something else entirely, a vast, icy landscape set against majestic mountains.

Peter reached out a hand to touch the door, and his hand met resistance. The yellow glow dimmed a little at his touch, and he pulled away, not wanting to leach any more of the power.

"It's a portal, but it doesn't want me. You said it spoke to you?"

Felicity had shrunken away from the arch while Peter was touching it, and she was now halfway across the room.

"Something about the mage council. 'Eligible for consideration' is what it told me." Felicity shuddered. "I don't want that. It can go away. I don't want to be on it's silly council."

"Ah." Peter nodded in understanding. "That must be where Norman went, don't you think, Petunia?"

"I don't know and I don't care," the small dragon pouted. "I just want my coin back."

"You know," said Peter, "I could give you another coin to replace it…"

Petunia looked horrified at the concept. "Another coin? What if someone stole…" She spluttered for a moment, trying to think of something close to Peter's heart but failing, "…one of your shoes?"

"My shoe?"

"Yes! A shoe!" She latched onto her idea. "And I offered to give you another shoe to make up for it."

"Another shoe?" Peter stared at his feet, thinking that this was a bizarre comparison.

"Just one shoe. A brand new shoe to replace the one you lost."

"They wouldn't match," Peter said flatly.

"That's right," said Petunia. "They wouldn't match, even if they were the same type of shoe. They'd be uncomfortable and would fit differently, and they'd chafe. You'd get blisters. Remember how you moaned about it last time you got blisters? You were so noisy. 'Oh, Petunia, my new shoes gave me blisters,' you moaned. And this time it would be one foot, so you'd limp around like an old grouch." Petunia feigned an exaggerated limp on the carpet, pretending to be Peter. "That's what you were like. That's what it would be like for me to have a different coin…"

"Why wouldn't you replace both shoes at the same time," Peter mused.

"I would, but *somebody stole my coin!*"

Peter couldn't help himself—he started to laugh at the hilarious exchange, at Felicity's aghast expression, at the relief of knowing where Norman probably was.

He leant against the wall, laughing until his sides hurt, laughing until the tears poured from his eyes, laughing until he was bent almost double, wheezing and heaving, unable to stop.

Only Felicity noticed, with some alarm, the lights brightening from Peter's touch.

"If you can't fix my problem, you should go and fix your pet dragon's problem," she snapped. Stop messing up my house and do what you came to town for."

Suzie stepped forward, between Felicity (who retreated at the gargoyle's presence) and Petunia (who, rather taken aback at being called a 'pet' clambered up on Suzie's shoulder when it was presented).

Still giggling, Peter straightened up. "Right," he said. "Reginald. Let's visit the butcher and find out where his son is."

Loud voices filled the air as the three approached the butchery, and Suzie moved to block Peter from approaching the front door.

"What? Suzie, get out of the way, we need to be in there!"

The stone cat shook her head slightly, blocking him further as he tried to bypass her.

"Suzie says we need to go by a different door," said Petunia gravely. "People don't sound happy."

Indeed, the voices coming from inside didn't sound at all happy. A shrill voice was yelling about someone being a drunken waste, a deep voice was yelling about money, and a whining voice was yelling about things not being his fault. Loud thwacks accompanied pain noises and someone was crying for Da to stop.

Suzie had moved towards the back of the building and was looking intently at the cellar entrance. Petunia fluttered her way over to the gargoyle.

"Suzie says there's something here we need to look at."

"Suzie doesn't say anything," Peter groaned. "She can't talk."

Petunia looked at him as if he was missing the obvious. "You don't need to talk to say things, silly." Turning her attention back to the cellar door, she cocked her head. "Suzie doesn't talk using a voice. And she's right, we need to open this door, and we need to do it now."

With a huff, Peter trod heavily towards the cellar door. "Sure. What's so important about this door anyway?"

Petunia looked up at him, a wild look on her tiny face.

"It's important because I can hear a dragon inside. I think it's my mother."

Chapter 21

661 OM Tarandeer
Year of the Tangled Briar

Pugton

The cellar door wasn't locked. Not even bolted. But that didn't help Petunia — the door was heavier than she was and she knew she could never lift it.

The mournful dirge floating out from below sang in a tune both too high and too low for Peter to hear, Petunia knew — she had long ago determined how deaf he was with his narrow band of hearing — but the words continued in a language that Petunia had not heard in 8 years:

> *All my get are destroyed*
> *My eyes are clouded in darkness*
> *Blood coats my stunted tongue*
> *I am bereft of any hope*
> *That I will ever dance the stars again*
> *Or watch the mist fade in the sun*
> *Chained here into this place…*

"Please, Peter, hurry. I can hear her. She's still down there!"

Peter moved so slowly! But eventually, the door was lifted, and Petunia flew down the stairs with all the speed her tiny wings could muster.

The smell was powerful to her sensitive nose. Blood and iron, offal, rank flesh, soiled hay, salt, charred wood... it was a wall of odour and ordure. It was all she could do not to gag as she descended into the darkness.

She remembered this place, even if there was no light to see by. At the bottom would be the butchery storage area, hanging flayed animal corpses and benches to store the innards, with two doors set into the earthen walls. She had never seen the other side of the door on the left, but the one on the right would lead to her mother. She wove her way through the hanging carcasses to the door she could hear the singing behind.

"Here, Peter, hurry!" she called out to the lagging boy. He was so slow! He was still only halfway down the stairs.

"I can't see," he complained. "Where are you?"

Petunia let out a brief spout of flame, lighting the room, singeing a cow corpse that hung from a hook nearby. The smell of roasting beef added itself to the cacophony of scent.

In the brief flash of light, Petunia noted that the earthen wall lacked from maintenance, and had crumbled near the wooden ceiling. A small gap next to a timber beam led its way straight through to the next room, so rather than waiting for Peter, she squeezed her way into the hole.

There was the furnace that led to the chimney that heated the butchery above.

There were the shackles that held down her mother and forced her to stillness so she couldn't flee.

There was her mother. Golden scales peeling. Her ribcage showing. Her belly shrunken. Tail amputated. Wings... wings twisted. Wings ragged. Incomprehensibly altered.

Those wings were broken. They had been twirled into fantastical shapes by pliers and hammers and heat until they stood up and out from the body beneath. They could no longer fold themselves onto the wasted body beneath them.

And more — those impossible wings were forced into such a shape that they would never fit through the door that Peter had not yet opened.

But here was her mother and she would be free. Petunia scrabbled her body the rest of the way through the hole, dove to the shackles.

"I'm here, mother, I'm here," she sang in Draconian.

Then she began to bite at the iron that held her mother's head in place, carefully heating the metal to soften it then gulping it down, huge shards that she didn't even bother to chew. She was halfway through the neck shackle by the time Peter finally managed to get the door open, Suzie pushing him forwards impatiently. And then Suzie was there beside her, stamping concussive blasts onto the leg shackles to break the metal close to spots of rust, and then Peter was on the other side, moving the stiff bolts out of the latches of the shackles on the other side until her mother was suddenly able to move.

And she did. Her first movements were to those shackles that had held her down, and she bit into them, chewing the iron while her teeth splintered on the metal, brittle from years of malnutrition.

And then she looked at Petunia, laying eyes for the first time on her child.

"I had thought you lost."

"I thought the same."

And then they caressed, nose to nose, taking in each other's scent.

Peter watched the two dragons nuzzle at each other like cats, wondering exactly how he was going to get this wagon-sized creature out of the room, let alone back to the tower.

After a moment, he decided to interrupt the touching scene.

"Ahem," he began, trying to get Petunia's attention. "Hate to state the obvious, but this other dragon won't fit through the door. Even if I could get it to the next room—say knock out the door, take down the wall—there's no way it would fit through the cellar entrance."

Suzie cocked her head in that annoying way she had of telling him he was missing something obvious. He ignored her and looked at Petunia. "What's your plan?"

The two dragons looked at each other. He felt like there were things he should be hearing but wasn't, in the same sort of way as when someone is moving behind you but you can't quite see them. He heard occasional clicks, groans and whistles from their direction, but nothing that sounded like real talking.

"You have to cut my wings off, human," the larger dragon said, turning its attention on him. Its voice was rough and hard to understand, as if talking with a mouth full of marbles.

"I… what?"

"Use the large cleaver. It is kept quite sharp—I am familiar with its bite. It may take effort, but it will sever my flesh. You may need my daughter's help with the bones, however."

"Suzie, will you help too?" Petunia asked, her voice trembling.

The stone cat immediately bowed toward the wing on the far side of the dragon's body and used teeth to saw at the base of the wing.

The larger dragon lowered its head, hissing in pain.

A sick feeling bubbled inside Peter's gut, but he turned and stepped back through that door, looking for the largest cleaver on offer amongst the carcasses.

But there… something better leaning against the wall. Not a cleaver. An axe, and a hard cylinder of tree stump to support and stabilise the wing as he was removing it. He moved the stump, rolling it back through the door and under the wing.

"What are you doing?" Petunia asked.

"I'll be back in a tick," Peter replied, running back to the axe while his courage remained.

He lifted it from its spot against the wall, feeling its weight—the smooth handle, the cold head, the balance. He ran his fingers against the edge, checking that it was sharp enough, then, with thunder in his ears, he rushed back inside and lifted the axe.

The dragon looked at him with wide, scared eyes as the axe came down, and suddenly screeches and howls filled the air as the axe bit hard into the metal bones of the wing. Bit, but not severed. And so, once more, the axe had to be wrenched from its place and brought down, hard, seeking to remove the metal wing in its entirety.

In his mind, Peter tried to imagine this was just another log he was chopping for wood, and his long practice meant that his strikes hit true and hit hard, but as the wing fell away from the log below it, the gush of silver fluid was like no log he had ever cut.

He dropped the axe, both hands hurrying to stem the flow, and as he did a tickle rose in the back of his neck, spreading through his head and arms like a winter chill.

The hot silver tide stopped pumping into his hands, and without stopping to breathe, he rolled the log to the other side and lifted the axe again.

Chapter 22

653 OM Tarandeer
Year of the Leaping Rabbit

Bakar

The books Peter had been reading swam in his head as he leant out over the balcony, tired. Almost two weeks into his sojourn into the sea of ink, the sound of the waves and the smell of the salt on the wind were now intertwined with his disconnection from the literature, and he relished each evening when he got a few moments of this unending landscape before sleep.

Last night he had seen a shape so vast that, when it broached the waves, it had blotted out the rising moon. It had seemed to be a fish, but something deep inside him suggested that it might be a beast of heat rather than cold and scales. The night previous, the dark water had been lit with thousands of pale, slightly glowing shapes, like undulating glassy bowls, all moving with one purpose for an unfathomable cause. Two nights ago, he had seen winged fish leaping from the water, trying to touch the sky. This place that looked so empty teemed with life, and every time he looked, he saw something new and wondrous.

The movement of the waves was mesmerising, and he could

feel the tension inside him settle every time he stepped out onto this tiny balcony.

Thirteen days into his time at Bakar and he was still no closer to touching his magic. He enjoyed his time with Chance — they took stolen moments to play marbles or scratch games of tic-tac-toe onto their slates, but the books were like a grindstone against his mind, and at the end of each day he felt that, rather than honing the keen edge, he was wearing away every shred of motivation.

He missed the feel of stretching his muscles, climbing trees, exploring. Even chores like chopping wood, carting water, digging the garden, washing dishes. Reading books every day left him more exhausted than he could have ever imagined, and his neck was sore from leaning over the table.

The books he had been studying talked about building magic potential, using terms like 'magic siphon', 'potential elevation', 'energy pump'. The methods all seemed to boil down to repetitive tasks. One mage danced in circles to pull the energy from the vortex he created. Another chanted the same tone over and over, absorbing the vibration of the air. A third he had read about just today counted beads on a string, shuffling them in her hand. Some threw themselves into community activities, helping the sick or elderly, others isolated themselves from everything, disappearing into caves in the wilderness.

Peter wondered why he couldn't just use his everyday chores to build these effects. Swinging an axe was a high-energy task, after all. If he could draw it from the splitting of the wood, from the crunch of his feet on gravel, from lifting and hauling, being mindful in his movements, perhaps he could avoid all these books in his future.

Chapter 23

661 OM Tarandeer
Year of the Tangled Briar

Pugton

The low keening coming from the dragon's mouth almost covered up the noise coming from the next room — the heavy tread of shoes on the squeaky stairs, the soft, mumbled swearing, bottles clinking as whoever it was bumped into shelving.

Peter placed a finger to his lips, hoping that silence could dissuade the presence in the other room from entering this one.

"That bloody racket," the garbled voice called. "Do I need to take that tongue out yet again? Bloody thing regrows, but do you think I care? I'll cut it so long as you keep making noise, you know." As the voice came closer, Peter stepped into the shadows beside the door, motioning for Petunia and Suzie to do the same.

The larger dragon, wise to this game, lay its head down where it had lain for so long, then froze, motionless, but still unable to control the moans of pain.

The door swung open, and Peter was shocked to see Reginald's face mottled and swollen with fresh bruises, his nose mashed across his cheek, blood still dripping over his mouth and chin. He held a large butcher's knife in his hand and was having difficulties balancing as he tried with the other hand to simultaneously tuck a large pair of pliers into his belt while trying to pull his sagging trousers up. His head was down, more focussed on what he was doing than looking ahead at the room.

"It's all your fault, stupid dragon. Stupid egg. Stupid." His voice raised in a mockery of someone else, "Reggie, you cost us so much money. Reggie, we could have been rich. Reggie, you need to do this, do that, be different..."

He lost his struggle with his trousers and the weight of the pliers on the belt pulled them all the way down. Bending unsteadily to right them, Reginald fell headfirst to the floor then rolled onto his side, still fighting with the pants to cover his now naked rear end.

In doing so, his head hit the edge of a propped up wing, which slowly teetered, then suddenly fell next to the drunken teen's head.

"Wha..."

Slowly his muddled mind processed that something was not as expected in the room, just as Peter stepped forward, feet directly in front of Reginald's bloody face.

"You can't be here," Reginald groaned. "What are you doing?"

"I'm taking this dragon," Peter said steadily. "Are you going to be a problem for me?"

A look of fear passed over Reginald's face. "You can't. He'll kill me. He'll actually kill me."

"Who?" Peter asked.

"Da." Reginald clutched at Peter's leg. "Please. He'll blame me. He blames me for everything. I'll die."

The dragon blinked. "He tortured me. He killed my children. He *should* die."

Reginald howled. "I didn't mean to. I was only ten. I thought they were worms!"

Peter looked at the pathetic person on the ground. "That

doesn't excuse torture." He pulled the lacing out of the neck of his tunic and began to tie Reginald's hands behind his back. "I'm not responsible for what your father does to you. If I were you, I'd be very quiet while we leave, then I'd leave too. Go somewhere—anywhere, but don't stay here. Don't stay in Pugton. You shouldn't stay where someone beats you."

At the dragon's request, Peter picked up the heavy wings, and they quietly left a crying Reginald behind.

Chapter 24

661 OM Tarandeer
Year of the Tangled Briar

Pugton

There were secrets to the wagon that Suzie apparently kept to herself, and Peter was surprised when she quickly set it to a closed carriage that had more space in the back than appeared possible from outside. As Suzie appeared to have all in hand (or paw? foot? mouth, even?), Peter sequestered himself in the back, more concerned with his unexpected new companion than with the way home.

"I am so sorry about your wings," he started, but was interrupted.

"They were useless. You did me a great service. Now, with a proper diet, I can grow new wings. My tail will return. In fact, if I'm not having to eat corpses on a daily basis, my tongue may even regain its full range of speech again."

Then the dragon took a bite of one of its detached wings. *Ew*, Peter thought, but tried hard to keep the disgust from showing on his face.

Petunia was flitting about, excited. Peter was puzzled at her new behaviour; she was making creaks and groans, clicking her tongue—he had never heard such sounds from her before.

"What are all of these noises you're making?"

"Oh, sorry, I'm talking in Draconid. You don't know Draconid. I should really translate, right?"

The larger dragon stopped its chewing. "My child tells me your name is Peter. You will probably never be able to pronounce my name, but an approximate translation is *The Sun Shines on the Misty Valleys and Burns Away the Shadow.* Humans used to call me Sunny. Given that my recent history has been less than pleasant, I prefer you shorten my name to Misty."

"And you're Petunia's mother?"

"Petunia? Is that what she told you her name is?" Misty chuckled. "The simplicity of children. The translation of her name amounts to *The Blossom of the One Who Offers Life.* But those words consist greatly of tones unavailable to your narrow band of hearing.

"Yes, I am Petunia's mother. Thank you for helping her to free me from captivity. It has been many years since I have been able to stretch my neck.

"Petunia has informed me that you are one of her pet wizards, and she suggests that I lodge with a third that she says is almost a dragon. If this is true, I would be honoured to meet the Scarred One she speaks of."

"Pet wizard?" Peter had often heard Norman tell him that Petunia was not a pet, but had never considered that he might be considered one himself. "She called me a pet?"

Petunia settled on Misty's broad shoulder. "Not in those exact words..." she said awkwardly. The words that followed tumbled out in a rush, "...But we really need to take Misty to see Scaramond. He'll help her get strong again, and he'll feed her good metal, and he'll give her a space to grow, and he likes dragons, and he even speaks a little bit of dragon..." These last words were a revelation to Peter, and he wondered what sort of things Scaramond had been telling the impressionable wyrmling.

"How about we just get to the tower first, and get your

mother to safety. We can think about next steps then."

While he and Petunia had been speaking, Misty had settled back into eating wings.

"What is going on here?" he asked, unable to continue ignoring the action. "I just don't understand. Why would you eat your old body parts?"

"Metal," Misty replied around bites. "I've been starved of metal for a long time, forced to eat meat creatures."

Petunia piped up as Misty turned her attention back to her act of cannibalism, "We're made of metal. Alloys and elements all in different places. You're made of meat, and you eat meat. We're made of metal, and we eat metal. Meat is yucky. I suppose we could eat it if we had to, but it wouldn't be nice."

"The one you let live, Reggie, complained about the stink and the mess," Misty grumbled around her meal, "But they wouldn't listen when I asked for a nice bit of iron or a morsel of copper. It's the teeth, I think. They look at sharp teeth and think 'carnivore' instead of 'metallivore'. Humans are such ignorant bumpkins."

"Well, thanks," said Peter with a sour note of sarcasm.

"Don't take my words badly, mage. You're not human."

"I... what? Of course I'm human."

"Mages aren't human. They look similar, but there are complications. Surely you have storyhoards amongst you that preserve the histories?"

This was a new term to Peter. He tried, but failed, to comprehend the turn of the conversation.

"I have no idea what you're talking about. Are you talking about books? Scaramond's library is big, but I don't remember seeing anything about us not being human."

"This Scarred One? I think I should like to know him. We shall rest at your abode, then you shall take me to him."

Peter felt uneasy at the imperious tone he imagined in Misty's voice, the strange things she was talking about, Petunia's constant twittering in a way he couldn't understand, and the way they referred to Scaramond…

"Petunia, why are you calling Scaramond 'The Scarred One'? He's so young and his skin is perfect."

"He has a million cuts, Peter. You see perfection, but all of his scars have joined together so that there is no place that is clean. He is made of scars."

Chapter 25

653 OM Tarandeer
Year of the Leaping Rabbit

Bakar

Day 14 was here. Mixed feelings assailed the boy as he prepared his meagre store of things to leave. He was pleased to be removed from the drudgery of books and squinting. The letters seemed to wriggle at him, taunting him as he tried to capture their meaning. His eyes would skip entire lines, he found, leaving him frequently confused and searching back through text for the things he had missed.

He was, however, sad to be leaving Chance. Sad to be leaving this amazing bedroom. Especially sad to be saying goodbye to the heaving mass of water that roiled beneath the tiny balcony.

His tiny pack neatly folded, he made his way to the dining hall for breakfast.

As always, a feast, prepared for the precise dietary needs of each attendant. He wondered how Chance and Master Scaramond remained so thin with so much food, but was far too polite to ask. He was sure he had gained weight in the past fortnight—the string on his pants waist seemed shorter when he tied it today than it used to, and the fabric stretched uncomfortably across the thighs when he sat.

"Petunia," he addressed the tiny wyrmling, who had been spending most of her time with Norman or Scaramond, "You've grown so much! Just two weeks ago, nose to tail, you were the length of my palm. You are twice as long now!" Not only that, but could he now see her wings with the naked eye, and she could use them to lift her body. She did just that, flying gracefully across to him.

"Yes!" he heard her faint voice say from in front of him. "I'm big now! Flying is fun."

Scaramond chuckled. "I intentionally fed her a rich diet, hoping for fast growth. Normally she would be with her mother for the first century, but without that protection she has to grow quickly. Bring her along next year, and we'll do the same again."

"Next year?" Peter was surprised. He had thought this a one time only visit.

"Yes, Peter," Norman said. "Apprentices need a full range of experiences. You can't be expected to know how to interact with the world if you only live with me in my tower. We go home for two weeks, then we will go abroad to visit a mage—I believe we will be headed south to Jerros. Then home for another two weeks, where we'll get visited by others, and then off to another mage. And so on. I'll try and get you interacting with as many other apprentices as possible, so you have some connections when your apprenticeship finishes. No use sending you out into a life where you know nothing and nobody. It's going to be eight years of work for both of us—you're not just going to be loafing around the tower. Scaramond and I have discussed your situation. Because you're a very special case, and because you and Chance seem to be getting along well, we've decided that this is going to be an annual visit. Petunia is to join us on these occasions, as Scaramond is quite well versed in Draconian physiology. It is a particular interest of his."

Chance beamed at the news that he would be seeing Peter again, and Petunia tried to fly a backward somersault but stalled mid-way through the flight. A cushion of air saved her from falling and Peter looked over to see Scaramond heavily pricking his thumb on the ornate pin he had been gifted.

"Careful, little flower. You don't have enough strength for that type of trick yet, and your wings are easily damaged. Remember to preen them regularly to make certain the bones stay straight."

Peter was alarmed. "You mean they might not? Bones are hard, aren't they?"

Scaramond redirected his intense gaze to focus on Peter. "Petunia's bones are made of metal. That means that when she is this small, they're like tiny wires, and wires can be bent. They require constant attention, which most wyrmlings would normally get from their mother, but Petunia will have to do herself.

"I expect you to provide her with a range of metals throughout the year. She needs a diet of iron, copper, tin, lead, nickel, zinc, and if you can find bauxite — it will naturally occur as a red rock, I have samples I can show you — that will give her access to aluminium as well. You may be able to find alloys that will give her sufficient combinations of these — brass, bronze, pewter, and the like. Other, more expensive, metals should be provided when you are able, especially if you can obtain sodium, magnesium, and potassium, which will heighten her breath attack, and manganese and mercury for flexibility and mental prowess. I am able to provide a range of rarer metals when Petunia visits, far beyond what a dragon her age would normally have access to."

The rest of the morning was spent recounting the books he had read and the methods he had taken from them, as well as his ideas around how to apply those methods. Scaramond nodded thoughtfully when Peter suggested mindfulness while he was conducting chores, in direct opposition to Norman's look of scepticism.

"The room you chose, the presence of the sea. How did that make you feel?" Scaramond interrupted at one point.

"Relaxed, sir. It was like I was being filled up with gentleness."

The tall mage nodded, then motioned Peter to continue his discussion of his learnings. Towards the end, when Peter was wrapping up, Scaramond leaned over to Norman. "Take him to the seaside as often as you can, I think. He may find that that a boon. Hydro-siphon from what I've witnessed."

Norman's eyes raised. "Really? Good thing we're off to Jerros then, I suppose."

"What's a hydro-siphon?" Peter was determined that they wouldn't get away with talking about him as if he wasn't there.

"There's a whole lot of study I'll be preparing for next year about planetary motion, how that interacts with the moon, and fluid currents that result from those things, but to put it in the simplest terms, you get power from the movement of water. The other things you discussed will be important as well, particularly the mindfulness aspect, but in the long run you may find that water and waves provide you with a steady stream of the power you need."

After an early lunch, the wagon was prepared for the long ride home. Chance stepped up to Suzie and looked her in the eyes for a long time, resting a hand on her stony shoulder. Then he leapt across to Peter and gave him a long, tight hug. Peter hugged him back just as tightly.

"I'll write often," he whispered.

Chance nodded before releasing him.

Then Master Scaramond stepped forward, and bent onto one knee so he could look Peter in the eye.

"It has been good to meet you. I believe you are bound for

big things.

"I want to thank you most of all for this pin that you gave me. It has been a long time since I have been gifted anything, and I would like to return the favour." He held out a small, flat ring in his hand that seemed to be made of some sort of ceramic. "I'll let you explore this at your leisure. There are secrets in it for you to discover, just as you have given me secrets to discover in this pin."

Then he rose and walked back into the tower. Chance wavered between staying and following, until some internalised pressure popped inside him and he ran to follow his master, waving wildly behind at the party of four.

Then Norman, Suzie, Peter and Petunia set off home, back to the tower in the woods.

Chapter 26

661 OM Tarandeer

Year of the Tangled Briar

Pugton

Da really will kill me this time, Reginald thought as he heard the door to the cellar close. *He'll find me down here and it won't be a fist, nor a belt. He'll grab a cleaver. He'll grab a cleaver and he'll hack me and then he'll hang the carcass and sell the meat.* He tugged on the ties, but they were secure, no give. It was like he was bound by wire.

Everything hurt. His face, his arms, his still bare arse where it scraped on the stone. His breath caught as he moved, telling him that he probably had a couple of broken ribs again.

It's my fault. I should never have killed those worms when I was a kid. I should have known what they were. We'd be rich by now. Da says he'd have sold them all and we'd be rich. Then Da wouldn't hit me anymore. And now that guy stole our dragon and Da will blame me and he'll get angry, and then he'll get what money he can from me. He'll sell my meat. Give it a fancy name and sell my meat. I'll be dead.

Reginald tugged on the wrist ties again, expecting there, like before, to be no movement. A flash of hope ran across his mind as a tiny bit of play emerged.

That guy was right. I'll need to run. I'll need to go to another town and start again. Go to where Da won't find me. Then I can find his dragon. He'll forgive me if I bring his dragon back.

The play in the ties was increasing, and Reginald smiled. *Maybe my luck's looking up. I'll be out of these things in a few minutes. And I'm even feeling a little better than I was before. Just a bruise on my side, not broken ribs.*

Just ten minutes after Peter had closed the cellar door behind them, Reginald's ties had loosed themselves. Reginald grabbed the axe Peter had left on the floor, and one of his father's knives, using the length of cord Peter had tied him with to hitch his pants up. He stretched, feeling better than he had in months, then slipped outside, staying quiet and low, avoiding people, and headed for the edge of town.

Chapter 27

661 OM Tarandeer
Year of the Tangled Briar

Norman's Tower

Peter half-expected Norman to come striding out of the tower, asking where he had been, but all was quiet. The tower was in its usual place, the afternoon sun was glimmering through the trees, tiny sparrows were picking away at the small vegetable garden he tended on a daily basis. The sharp woodsmoke scent still lingered in the air, the wreck of Petunia's bush a black patch on the ground.

Peter put a hand over his eyes. "Petunia, we forgot. Your coin. We didn't get it. He was right there and we didn't get it."

Petunia perched on the top of the well, looking over at the place her hoard used to lie. "It's okay. I got something more precious than my coin today. We'll go find Reginald some other time and get it."

Misty tilted a quizzical head and shot some quick clicks and squeals at Petunia, who replied, also in Draconian. Then Misty took a deep sniff of the air.

"If you're looking for the thief, there's no use chasing the Reggie boy. He may be guilty of much, but in this he is innocent.

There is none of his stench here—I know it far too well and it thankfully does not taint this air."

Peter rounded on Petunia. "I thought you said it was Reginald who took your coin!"

Petunia looked ashamed. "I know. I did. He was the only person I could think of. But it's okay! We found my mother! That makes it all better."

"Doing something bad doesn't get evened out by doing something good. Life isn't like that. There are no scales to weigh things on. You were going to accuse him of stealing when he didn't do it. He may be a horrible person and deserved bad things, but what if he wasn't? I'm glad you found your mum. But lying isn't okay."

Peter marched inside and pulled out Petunia's hoard from his drawer. "Where do you want your things?" he called out, feeling the anger bubble inside him.

Petunia had followed him inside, and her small, abashed voice came from behind him. "I don't want any of it anymore. Give it all to Misty. She needs every piece of my hoard to get better."

He gathered the small cache of metal together, then went through his other drawers, pulling aglets and metal beads off his clothing wherever he found them. A couple of low denomination coins were added, then he tossed everything into a small brass vase and carried it out to Misty.

"Petunia's hoard is here, along with a few bits and pieces of mine. It's not much, but it's what I can part with. I'm sure when Norman gets back he'll be able to add more."

"My thanks, mage. This is a rich feast in comparison to the meals I have eaten over the last decade.

"You should treat Petunia less harshly. Tell me, at what age does one of your children become an adult?"

"Eighteen. Why?"

"I want you to remember that Petunia will not be considered

an adult until she is 100. She is roughly as mature as one of your two-year-old children. She may have your language and seem older than she is, but she is a baby still."

Peter sighed. "I know. I just forget sometimes. Norman treats her like an adult, so it's hard to look at her and see a baby. I'll apologise for snapping at her.

"She's right about Scaramond, though. You will be in a place where you can have consistent access to the metals you need, and he'll treat you very well. I'll send Suzie to Bakar in the morning to get him."

Chapter 28

661 OM Tarandeer

Year of the Tangled Briar

Atinien Mountain

Morning arrived, as it had a habit of doing. Norman dragged himself out of the tiny bed, saw to his ablutions, and approached his mentor's room.

He stopped short of opening the door when he heard voices within.

"…wasn't too difficult to hear, I hope?" Albert's reedy tones were muffled through the thin door, contrasting with a strong but gentle tenor.

"I've heard many such speeches before, young man, and I will hear them again. Harder to handle when I was younger, I think. Each of our gifts bears its own cross, and this is mine."

"He'll need support, you know. I hope you'll help him. His views may not be…" a fit of coughing interrupted the conversation. "Change. He'll bring change."

"It's nothing I won't have seen before. There is very little I haven't seen. He'll have my support, if he'll take it. I don't think he likes me much…"

Feeling a little embarrassed at hearing the obviously sensitive conversation, Norman removed himself, donning furs and stepping outside to grab a helping of stew.

Some overzealous mage had been fiddling with the weather overnight, and he stepped into a balmy 10°C. Mages were standing about in the sunshine wearing light coats instead of the heavier garments of the day before. Norman sighed heavily and tapped an older mage on the shoulder.

"Gantry, you're familiar with stone magic. This area never gets this warm and we're on an old volcanic plug. Can you stabilise the rock face for me? This heat is dangerous and we'll get rockfalls by mid-morning if it's not addressed."

It was obvious that there had been heavy traffic to and from the succession box overnight, the way now trodden deeply into mud. With a thought, he gathered hay from a farmer near Pugton — someone he knew wouldn't mind, so long as he paid when they next saw each other.

Scaramond appeared next to him, approaching from behind. "I was about to get to that, but you beat me to the punch. I'll get someone to lay the hay out. You need to eat, remember?"

Norman nodded. "Thanks. I got distracted by the heat. I had Gantry do some of his stonework just to make certain we didn't get any slippage, by the way, so that's one problem you shouldn't need to worry about."

"Good call. The temperature has risen quite sharply, hasn't it? Do I need to check on that privy?"

For the next ten minutes, the two continued to discuss the challenges of the weather change, then Norman continued on his way to breakfast. The porridge he pulled out was sweet and tasty, so he grabbed a second bowl for Albert and took it back inside.

Albert was alert and sitting up, bright-eyed. He tsked at the sight of the bowl in Norman's hand.

"Scaramond brought me a bowl this morning already," he said. "I haven't the appetite for more."

Norman saw that there was a full bowl of something

smooth and grey cooling on the bedside table, a spoon still sitting in the mash.

"Wheat porridge with blueberries. Just the thing." Albert smiled.

Norman frowned. "Looks like you've barely touched it. You need to eat."

"Pish." A round of coughing left the old mage breathing heavily with tears leaking from the corners of his eyes. A trembling hand lifted to wipe his face. "I don't get hunger like I used to. A little taste is enough.

"So how's the mood outside? Any grumbles?"

Norman sat and discussed the weather, the people, world politics. At times he noticed that Albert was dozing, but he continued his stream of conversation, as Albert occasionally lifted a hand to indicate he should keep going. Towards mid-morning, a chime interrupted him, and he stopped to listen. Albert's eyes popped open.

"That's the end of the submission period. You'd better get out there to hear results."

Norman nodded and moved outside, only to see Highmage Foljur removing a piece of paper that had spat itself out of the box at his touch. The twelve men who had sat on the council table the night before gathered solemnly together and filed past him into the mountain.

He turned, curious, intending to follow, but was held back by a hand on his shoulder.

"You can't be in there right now. That's council business. They won't take long."

The youthful face of Scaramond looked down at him. "I've been to a few of these. It never takes more than 20 minutes to deliberate. You should find yourself a good seat in the hall before all the best spots are taken. I'm too old to be in the running, so I'll sit with Albert while everyone else is busy."

The red-robed mage walked away, leaving Norman to

wonder just how old this mage really was.

Chapter 29

661 OM Tarandeer
Year of the Tangled Briar

Atinien Mountain

The time moved quickly, but with a dreadful slowness. The noise in the hall surrounded Norman like a cocoon, the muttered conversations combining to a roar of sound. He felt apart from the mob, even as he was knocked by bodies and jostled by elbows. The room was packed with rows of chairs, where last night there had been tables. Slowly he worked himself to the front of the room, the first rows before the tiny stage thankfully bare of people, the sound a little less oppressing.

There he sat, waiting, staring at the wood-grain of the polished floor beneath his feet, tracing its whorls and lines with his eyes, seeking a measure of quiet in his mind. And so, entranced, he barely noticed when the room around him quietened. It was only when a body sat down beside him that he looked up to see the council had taken their seats on the stage, with the silk-clad Bellamy standing at a podium.

"As is customary, we were presented with five names from the succession box, in order of suitability for a role on the council. We are offered five names rather than one so that we are able to reject candidates that are impolitic — for example mass murderers and the like..." A mutter broke out, and Bellamy held up a hand for quiet. "This is also so that a candidate who has changed their mind about being on the council can refuse their candidacy if offered, without the process having to start again.

"We have conferred with each other and find unanimously that there is no impediment to the first candidate's membership to the council. We call upon Norman Linter to step forth."

A chill prickled over Norman's skin in that moment, and he hesitantly rose, half convinced that he had imagined his name. But as the eyes of the twelve Highmages looked down on him, he took a deep breath and stepped forward.

"I'm Norman Linter. That's me."

One of the Highmages helped him onto the stage and motioned for him to approach Highmage Foljur.

"Norman Linter, are you satisfied to take oaths of office to join the Highmage Council?"

Norman nodded.

"Out loud, please, unless there is an impediment to your voice," Bellamy whispered.

"Y-yes," Norman stumbled, his throat dry and his voice unexpectedly raspy. "I will take the oaths."

"Norman Linter, do you swear to serve the Highmage Council all the days of your life to the best of your ability?"

"I do."

"Do you swear to uphold the values of the Highmage Council with truth, integrity, and honour?"

"I do."

Do you swear to work in the best interests of the people of Varthien, without bias or political intent?"

"I do."

"Then, I am pleased to announce our newest Highmage, Highmage Linter. Welcome to the council!"

A roar broke out across the hall like a wave of sound, and Norman found himself staring at a sea of faces who were all staring back at him. Then he was ushered from the stage by 11 other Highmages. Highmage Foljur remained at the podium for a moment.

"We will be breaking for a short while as Magus Tarandeer now announces his choice for the new Magus. Due to his frailty, this will occur in chambers, and we will present the incoming Magus once his choice has been established and witnessed."

Then he, too, departed the stage, and they trod their way through the crowd, out of the hall, and across to the mountain abode.

The mass of thirteen men barely fit into the small bedroom carved into the rock of the mountain, and Norman found himself squeezed up against the cold basalt. His gaze flicked across the faces of twelve sombre frowns, all peering down at the old man in the bed. Briefly, his mind swept to Peter, wondering how well the boy was fending for himself, but the thought was too beset upon by the other pressing concerns of the moment and was set aside.

The old man took a deep, rattling breath and Norman's attention focussed on him. The lined face was pale, almost greying with the illness that had ravaged him. The eyes were open now but squinting at the light that one of the mages had hung over the bed. A twitch of Albert's liver-spotted hand dimmed the light, causing a brief scowl to appear on the face of the culprit.

Norman was surprised to notice the cloudy edges of cataracts forming in Albert's eyes—how had he missed them since his arrival? And had it really been so long since he had visited? Truly, he had been engrossed in his tutelage of Peter, but this evidence of time's passage shocked him far more than the frailties he had already witnessed. Numbly, he reached down for Albert's hand, but finding it in the grip of the mage beside him, he settled for resting his hand upon the leathery arm, the touch of skin making him feel vaguely comforting and comforted in some slight way.

Another deep, wheezing breath came from the man in the bed, and on its heels, the choking, phlegm filled cough which had filled Norman's ears since early yesterday morning. One of the throng on the other side of the bed gently propped Albert up and the coughing fit subsided, the old man's head lolling on his neck as if the muscles had long given up from exhaustion.

"Oh, look," came the quiet voice, still panting from the brief exertion, "You're all here. Anyone would think it was my birthday!"

Titters sounded within the room, nervous, as if they feared the humour was inappropriate for them to respond to. Norman felt a smile tug at one cheek, the swift exhalation of air as a single puff of laughter escaped his tense chest.

"Well, I suppose we should get on with this," Albert wheezed when everyone had settled. "I'm not going to last all that long now, so I suppose naming my successor is in order. We all know it would have been young Theophrastus, but that episode with the dairy cow has rendered him somewhat... inappropriate... for the position."

The titters were louder this time, with some mutters in the back as someone explained the joke to their neighbour. A balding man toward the corner of the room was blushing quite badly, his eyes directed to the floor. Norman looked around at his new fellows, wondering which the title would fall to.

"I've thought on this for a few months now. Theo didn't really give me much time, did he? So, this decision will not sit well with everyone.

"Bellamy..."

The huge man who had been speaker both last night and on the stage today pushed his way through the throng, beaming.

"...is senior, but far too headstrong. Abercrombie..."

A thin, bookish man craned forward.

"...has also been within our number for some time, but

cannot make a decision to save his life."

The bookish man leaned back, displeasure souring his features. There was some whispering from the back, possibly from the same person who had been muttering earlier.

"There is, however, one of our number who once acted hastily to dreadful consequences and has since been much more circumspect about his decisions. When this man joined our ranks at the age of 44, he had already managed to release himself from the physical restraints of his ability and was working from mental capacity alone." This revelation raised a gasp among many of the assembled mages, some of whom were still bound to physical focuses centuries into their working. "He certainly has no issue with taking responsibility for his actions, which is a fine quality in a leader. He has experienced a great amount of change in his life, and perhaps because of this he refrains from puffing himself up, unlike many of our fellows; instead, he works quietly in the background for the betterment of society. He has also shown willingness to teach; his current apprentice is almost at their majority. Norman Linter, my boy, I name you as my successor."

As angry voices started to object, Norman just gaped in astonishment. Not even an hour into his role and he was being expected to take over. A feeling akin to being swallowed whole by a monstrous beast filled his chest and his vision blackened at the edges as his breath quickened.

"Me? But I'm not ready. I've only just been elected and you want me to run things? I can't..."

Albert pushed himself up in the bed. "This is my choice, and I have reasons for doing it. We're a bunch of old men who never do anything that doesn't increase our comfort. We don't move forward. You can take us in new directions and bring change to Varthien. I trust you to do that."

As soon as the others had filed out of the room, jostling each other and eying him darkly, Norman started fumbling in his pocket.

"I've got a solution," he said, "You don't have to die! We can get it all back; your youth, your health..."

With a flourish, he drew the small, forlorn-looking silver coin from his pocket. It was partially caked in dirt and had black tarnish marks in places.

"This," he waved the thing in the air, "is most remarkable. So much energy stored up in this one little piece of metal! There are texts that speak of this, but..."

Albert raised a hand to silence Norman's stream of words. "I suppose this is a hoard item then?"

Norman's excitement was brimming from him, and the word came out almost as a squeak, "Yes! The first!"

Albert frowned in understanding. "Ah. And did Petunia give this item up willingly? Did you tell her that it was to save me, or did you simply take it while she was unaware?"

"She would have allowed it if there had been time to wake her, but your summons was so urgent..." Norman said, slower now, wary. A bony, raised finger stopped him from speaking further.

"Ah."

Albert took the coin and inspected it... the blackened, muddy half that had been beneath the earth; the shiny, silver half that had been caressed so many times by the small draconian tongue. His hands trembled slightly, but whether it was from age or exhaustion Norman could not tell.

"This coin is indeed a powerful item. The love that has been lavished into this every day since that young wyrm received this is quite remarkable. It is not, however, powerful enough to give me my youth and my health, even if I wanted those things back. A stolen thing can never be that powerful."

Norman's shoulders sagged, disappointment creasing his face.

"Always remember that power lies in the asking and the giving. Taking has a power all of its own, but that is a hard, harsh power unless it is softened by gifting. Nonetheless, I thank you for the thought, but I think I'm quite prepared to deal with what comes next."

The old face split into a conspiratorial grin as he placed the coin carefully back into the centre of Norman's palm. "My life has been a little longer than most anyway. Did you know, I'm 739 this year?"

He chuckled. Then the chuckle became a cough. And another. And another. A cascade of coughs followed, and suddenly people began piling through the door again, concerned faces on every man.

As the coughing fit passed, Albert looked around. "Do you know," he finally wheezed between great, heaving gasps, "I do think we should have more women in our upper numbers…"

Chapter 30

1 OM Linter
Year of True Sight

Atinien Mountain

Norman was shuffled outside, pushed to the stage like a piece of furniture. His mind was a jumble of words and concepts that he had yet to fully grasp, and he stared into that sea of faces as Highmage Foljur spoke into the crowd with words that Norman couldn't process. Then, when that same Highmage turned to him and muttered "It's your turn, Norman. You need to name the new year," Norman stumbled forward, completely unprepared.

"Um. Some… some of you know that I was apprenticed to Magus… um, former Magus Tarandeer. But most of you never knew him, will never get a chance to… um…"

Norman didn't know what the words were as they tumbled out of his mouth. He felt as if he were spectating from inside his own body, some stranger working his arms, his legs, his mouth.

"Albert Tarandeer, when he found me, saw me more truly than any other person before in my life. I owe him a debt of gratitude. My life so far has been moulded by his influence. And so I would like to name my first year as Magus for him: The Year of True Sight."

Then he stepped away from the podium, still puppetted by some foreign internal impetus, down, away from the grasping hands and congratulating voices, and then was led to a dark, quiet place by a youthful face in carmine robes who sat him down and crouched before him.

"Breathe. That's all you need to do right now. Just breathe. Close your eyes. Let your mind drift."

Norman's eyes slowly focussed on the silver triskele the man before him wore, light playing on the smooth yellow stone set in the centre. He visually traced the unbroken line as it passed over itself, through itself, back onto itself, around and entwined in never ending loops. His breath, his heartbeat, his thoughts all steadied and slowed.

"This is all a show for those out there. They see a title, not a person. You're going to need help, just for a little while."

Norman nodded, still focussing on the silver against the red, unwilling to face anything other than the monotony of this thin, metal line.

"Albert asked me to support you, help you, just like I did for him when he first became Magus. I am happy to assist you, if that is what you wish."

The voice fell silent as Norman gathered his thoughts, then lifted his gaze.

"Exactly who are you, Scaramond? Just yesterday I thought you younger than I am, yet you helped Albert when he became Magus? Just how old are you?"

"I don't know. I've been around a while. I don't really remember how long; it gets fuzzy.

"But that really doesn't matter right now. What matters is you. There are a lot of people in that room right now, all wanting to get close to you, all wanting to influence you, and you need someone to shield you from the worst of it. I'm offering to be that shield."

"Are you one of those people that wants to influence me, Scaramond?"

"It's all part of the game, isn't it? Like I said, I've been around a while. I've seen a lot of things. Maybe I can steer you through some of the rough patches, warn you about some pitfalls. I don't want to be Magus. I just want stability."

Norman met the green eyes in that unlined face. "I'll think on it."

Then he stood and walked back to the mountain to sit once more at his mentor's side.

Chapter 31

REVERBERATION

1 OM Linter
Year of True Sight

Norman's Tower

Suzie had left early, unencumbered by cart or companions, bearing only a note in her stone gullet. And so, midmorning, there were only three inhabitants at the tower — Misty and Petunia sunning themselves while Peter saw to the garden.

The sound of the announcement echoed in the ears, seeming to come from everywhere and nowhere, in a voice that could not be pinpointed as male or female. The voice was familiar — Peter had heard it on the first day of the year every year he had been alive, announcing the name of the new year, but nobody had ever explained where the voice came from. He looked across at Petunia and Misty, who were listening intently as well.

A new Highmage has been appointed. Norman Linter has been announced Highmage.

Then, less than an hour later, while the three were still mulling over the words that had been uttered and what they meant for the future, the voice spoke again.

A new Magus has been appointed. Highmage Norman Linter has been announced Magus. One Our Mage Linter is the Year of True

Peter looked at Petunia with wide eyes. "Did I just hear right? Norman is the Magus?"

Petunia wittered happily. "Norman is the Magus," she sang, "He's the most important person. Then when you're old, you can be the Magus too. You're important. And you and Norman can be Magus together, and I can be Magus too..." She flew off to search for a new place to build her nest, singing about important people and how everyone was the Magus.

"It seems I have fallen into influential circles," mused Misty. "You are this Magus Linter's apprentice, are you not?"

"Yes. I didn't even know all this was happening. I just woke up yesterday morning and Norman was gone. No note. I worried myself sick about it. How could he become Magus and not even tell me? It seems like something I should have been told about."

Misty barked a short laugh. "Mages don't know when they're going to enter the council. Someone has to die for that to happen, and mages often live far beyond the lifespans of their human counterparts, so it's not that frequent. I doubt your Master Norman has future sight to know when people are going to die, so my conclusion is that this is probably as much a surprise to him as it is to you. I haven't heard the Death Dirge yet, so old Tarandeer is still hanging on, but he'll be gone soon."

Peter tugged on the small ceramic disc at his throat, deep in thought. He was a little offput by Misty's irreverence when talking about Magus Tarandeer, but decided to let it slide for the moment. He was too busy wondering if Norman would make it home for his birthday.

Chapter 32

1 OM Linter
The Year of True Sight

Atinien Mountain

"Ah. Magus," Albert wheezed as Norman entered the room. "I … suppose I should … stop calling you … 'Boy' now, eh?"

The breathy voice was halting and soft, filled with pauses, and Albert's chuckle at his own words devolved into a fit of coughing.

"I'll always be your 'Boy'. Titles are only for company, remember?"

"Sca… Sca…" The words struggled to make it out of Albert's mouth.

"Scaramond?"

Albert nodded, wiping his mouth with a trembling hand.

"He spoke to me a short while ago. Wanted to act as my shield, he said."

"Good advisor," Albert whispered. "Knows what's needed."

"I don't trust him." Norman turned and walked to the door, making certain that it was shut. "How can I trust him? His very face is a lie."

"You, of all people? Still wearing that prosthetic?"

Norman's hand raised to his face, feeling the wire frame that he had worn so long it had worked its way into his skin. He had almost forgotten it was there — he never took it off, even slept in it.

"That's different."

"Is it? You present yourself to the world a certain way, mould the image people see of you. So does he."

"But this is my face. I chose this face so that people could see who I actually am."

"Just so, boy. Just so."

Chapter 33

635 OM Tarandeer
Year of the Twirling Leaf

Parancy

"Come on, Norm, stop dragging your toes! How often do we get a day like this?"

Norman broke into a trot, trying to catch up. The day was, indeed, a good one: sun not too hot, wind not too cold, fête down the road, Gareth's company, and leave to spend a day and a pocket full of coin on whatsoever he chose.

"I was enjoying the trees," he shouted. "The mountain is just ice and snow. I don't get to see greenery very often."

Grabbing hold of the back of Gareth's shirt, he bent to the long grass and plucked a stem, which immediately went into his mouth.

"I can't even go to the privy without a slab of wool around me. With all of the magic Albert has I don't see why he can't just set up a portal we can *go* through."

"But where would the portal *go* to? You'd create a whole new mountain. A holiday destination for dung beetles!"

"A shit of a holiday that one would be!" The two boys fell against each other laughing, and were still laughing when they reached the outskirts of the fête, the bright ribbons showing the way waving gently in the wind.

They wove their way through the people, looking at the stalls and exhibits. Fresh fruit and vegetables sat alongside livestock, which sat next to games of ring toss, confectioners, waferers offering their fresh and hot pastries made on the spot.

Stopping for a moment to listen to a spruiker calling out about the grotesques, the two were approached by colourfully clad man.

"Sir," he addressed Gareth, showing the interior of a cape pinned with copper wire formed into rings, bracelets, and brooches, set with colourful glass beads. "Can I tempt you with my wares? Fine trinkets that you might give your lady beside you?"

Gareth stumbled at the use of the term 'lady'. "What? Um..."

Norman quickly lay a hand on Gareth's arm. "It's a common mistake. Happens all the time." He turned to the salesperson. "Don't be embarrassed, it's just that my beard hasn't grown in yet. Do you have anything that would suit a heavy cloak? Something masculine..."

Later, finding a quiet spot on a piece of grass to eat skewered beef strips, Gareth spoke around the piece of gristle in his mouth.

"I almost forgot, but that jeweller reminded me. I made you something." He wiped the greasy fingers of one hand onto his tunic, his other hand holding his dripping stick aloft as he reached for his satchel. He fumbled inside it for a second, then pulled out a thing made of wire and wool and tossed it to Norman. "Put it on."

Norman picked it up from his lap, looking at it curiously. "I would, but I don't know what it is."

"That's your beard. It just grew in."

Norman inspected the form. Thin gold wire hooks descended into spiralled forms with tiny tufts of wool. "Not much of a beard," he said.

"Psh. Put it on. Think about how you want your beard to look. One of the perks of being apprenticed to a shapechanger is that I've got a good idea about transformation magic. You may never be able to grow your own facial hair, but this at least will stop people from mistaking you for a girl."

Hesitantly, Norman settled the hooks over his ears, allowing the spiralled golden mesh to fit itself to his cheeks and chin.

"What now?" he asked.

"Now nothing," Gareth responded with a smile that almost split his face, and threw him a small mirror. "Just look."

Norman looked into the mirror and saw his face, jaw squarer than it had been, a fine growth of auburn hair on his cheeks, chin, and upper lip. Tears pricked in the back of his eyes as, for the first time, he saw his face as he wished it, not as it was. He lifted his gaze and looked at the younger boy with adoration.

"I don't know what to say. Thank you! I'll never take it off!"

Chapter 34

ONE NOTE SONG

1 OM Linter

The Year of True Sight

Atinien Mountain

Albert was sleeping. His breath rattled steadily, loud in the quietness of the room.

Norman found that noise soothing — a point of sameness in a world that had shifted so sharply under his feet. He allowed his mind to drift, simply being. He leant back in his chair, taking a moment to close his eyes and relax.

The lodge had emptied quickly after the announcement of his instatement, with only a few lagging. The rock had shaken with the thunder of a thousand mages teleporting away to their respective homes across Varthien. All was quiet now, nobody interrupting.

After a time, he woke. Something was different. The door remained closed, no sounds emanating from outside. All was silent.

All was silent.

Norman looked toward the bed, where the absence of Albert's breath was such an unnerving change that it had woken him. All was still. Unmoving.

Norman rose, reached out a hand, reached for Albert's wrist, felt for a pulse.

Unmoving.

"Albert?" he asked, "Albert, can you hear me?"

Silence.

He smoothed the hair away from Albert's face, the cooling skin still pliable, soft.

Then he lifted his head, opened his mouth, and sang the death dirge. Just a single note, filled with the pain and grief of losing one so close.

"Oooooooooooooooooo…"

Outside, the man sitting vigil in the hall opened his throat in the death dirge.

"Oooooooooooooooooo…"

One by one, the council members, hearing the call wherever they were on the mountain, lifted their voices in the same note.

"Oooooooooooooooooo…"

The sound passed through the portals of every mage who had been eligible for succession, and everywhere that call was heard, it was taken up.

"Oooooooooooooooooo…"

It floated on the wind, through the streets of villages, towns, and cities, until the sound was everywhere.

"Oooooooooooooooooo…"

The entirety of Varthien vibrated in time with this singular note. Everywhere, people together grieved the loss of the Magus who had guided magic for 661 years. The coastal Chirren took up the howl, clicking their chelicerae. The Talking Trees of Garthanien took up the call, shaking branches in creaks and groans. The Alven in the Northeastern Reaches woke from their huddles, each lifting their furred throats to croon the sound of death.

"Oooooooooooooooooo…"

When the low sound had passed, Norman dropped his head, only to see that Scaramond had entered the room, linen wraps piled high in his hands. He placed them onto the dresser, then carefully stripped back the top sheet from Albert's body, folding it into crisp, concertina folds at the foot of the bed.

The two men worked in concert, soft sponges cleaning the skin, gentle hands moving Albert's arms to cross over his chest, then together they took the lengths of linen and neatly swaddled his body from feet to neck, leaving only his head uncovered, pausing only to carefully fit the small mortuary knives to Albert's thumbs, that he might cut himself free in case of mistaken death diagnosis.

With a great heave, Norman pushed the wardrobe to the side, revealing the carved frame of a staircase leading down.

Then he broke the silence they had both adhered to all the way through the death rites. "The mausoleum. Albert told me it was down here."

With a fist covering the point of the long pin he wore at his breast, Scaramond lifted the body of the former Magus from the bed on an invisible platform, then forward, through the entrance, down the staircase, both men following behind.

Light flowed before them, a seamless bubble building the illusion of timelessness, each step an age. Then, long after his feet had grown sore and his breath had grown short, Norman saw the stairs end, stretching into an opening so vast that the bubble of light touched neither walls nor ceiling.

The body turned to the left, following the wall, still travelling before them. Norman gave a backwards look to the man behind him, then followed the body.

The way seemed less of an age now that the way was less vertical and more horizontal, or perhaps it was that the next entrance was so much closer than the way down the stairs had been. The entrance was surrounded in bright mosaics that gleamed in the sourceless light, flowing out along the floor in a river of tiny tiles. The body passed into the room beyond, and the light passed with it, leaving the two men momentarily in shadows before they, too, stepped through into the mausoleum.

A bowl of tiles was set into the wall to the right, and Scaramond took one, motioning for Norman to do the same. Then he stepped in front, one hand reaching for Albert's, drawing him to a low archway set into the wall.

Norman followed, flipping the tiny tile in his hand, looking at the tiles along the floor, the tiles along the wall, the other low archways set into the wall, each arch holding piles of rags and bones, each with a tiled name over the top, each with a vase of flowers, stems still green, each archway with divots in the tiles before it from hundreds of years of knees. And here, this low archway, empty, untiled, nameless. Scaramond took his tile of lapis, pressing it into the lettering that had been lightly traced onto the stone in chalk, the lettering that said 'Albert'. He motioned for Norman to do the same, and he did, feeling the buzz of the tile vibrating its way into the stone, the scent of Albert's magic bringing tears to his eyes.

"Why are you even still here?" he asked the tall man, angry that this person was intruding on these last moments.

"I always come to place my apprentices to their last rest," Scaramond answered. "You and I are the closest to family Albert has left. It is fitting that we two are here, that we two were his support in these last days."

"Your apprentice? How? Your face is unlined. You cannot possibly be so old. How?"

In response, Scaramond walked down the row of low arches, stopping only at the end.

"Excuse me, Annabelle, I shall only borrow this a moment," he said to the dusty pile, linen rotted away to nothing. He carefully lifted a bone, slipping the thumb-dagger off and carrying it to Norman.

He held it out to the younger mage.

"Here. Cut me exactly here, between the first and second finger of the left hand. As deep as you please—all effects from pain to this area will be non-harmful."

Norman frowned. "You want me to *cut* you?"

"Yes," said Scaramond. "I would ask this of no other, and under no ordinary circumstance, but as you are Magus now, you need to understand what I am. Cut me."

Hesitantly, Norman took the thumb-knife and drew it lightly over the webbing between the two fingers.

Scaramond pulled the flesh tight, stretching the skin so that the thin slice parted.

"Watch."

Within seconds, the cut was gone, wisps of magic knitting the skin back together. Norman looked up, a metallic copper smell in his nose, and could see blue wisps of magic colouring Scaramond's eyes, the blue glow of magic brightening the mosaics, the blaze of magic flowing in and around the hatpin Scaramond wore at his breast.

"I cannot age. Age leads to suffering. As I suffer, my gift heals the damage."

But Norman was fixated on the pin at the other mage's breast. A familiar pin.

Chapter 35

1 OM Linter
The Year of True Sight

Bakar

The great iron gate leading to the grounds of Scaramond's tower swung open at Suzie's approach. She looked up, examining the invisible threads of energy that had tripped the motion. A pulse of energy lit up a beam that travelled a path to the sixth floor of the main building. Satisfied that her presence had been announced to somebody within, she stepped through the gate.

The way had been a long one, and she desperately hoped for a few licks of magic. Usually she would not make such a lengthy trip alone, and while she had set off with a large amount of energy in reserve, she didn't think she could guarantee making it all the way back home without a little extra. Thankfully, Scaramond was usually a generous host to her, and would stockpile tailings throughout the year for her.

There was magic in the air here. Not only from the tower though—the vast grounds swirled with the intoxicating aroma—not for the first time did Suzie wish she had the opportunity to hunt out its source.

Ahead of her, Suzie saw the front door to the tower open, but rather than the familiar form of Scaramond, his apprentice mage emerged.

Suzie liked Chance. He didn't assume her compliance or take her for granted, perhaps because he had many similar constraints to her own. Plus, he was good for book recommendations — he read almost as voraciously as she did, and he was always eager to pile them up for her in the study.

A concerned look crossed over his face, and he approached her quickly, hands palm-side up in a query. In response, Suzie dropped the note directly at his feet and sat, awaiting him as he read the note.

Quickly scanning the note, Chance breathed deeply, then in a flurry of hand signals, communicated for Suzie to stay where she was, that he would come with her. The gargoyle cocked her head, puzzled that he wasn't fetching his master, but he gave a stop signal once again and ran back to the tower.

Minutes later, he came back, this time bearing his slate.

Scaramond's not here, he wrote. *I'll take us to Peter.*

But before either of them could make any further plans, a sound drifted on the air around them.

"Oooooooooooooooooo…"

Suzie immediately understood the ramifications of the Death Dirge on this day, following the announcements that had occurred earlier. In grief for Norman's loss, she closed her eyes and lifted her open mouth to the sky.

Chance nodded to her and lifted his voice in the same dirge. His voice rustled the leaves on the trees around them, whipped up the wind, and the voiceless Suzie was now howling her dirge too, as the moving air rushed past her mouth as though she were a panpipe.

After a long moment, the dirge died down and Chance and Suzie relaxed. The skinny teen looked at the stone cat next to him and a cheeky grin appeared on his face. He winked, tapping a forefinger against his nose, and said a single word.

"Peter."

An oval of golden light expanded next to him. With an elaborate flourish and bow, he motioned for Suzie to step through.

Suzie could taste the rich flavour of Chance's magic as she entered the portal, and then she was through, standing next to the well beside the tower she called home.

Peter was there, looking surprised at her sudden appearance, then even more surprised as Chance appeared behind her. She looked to Chance, and he motioned her to the still active portal, which she hungrily drank until the portal dissolved, glad to have immediate sustenance. She looked over in gratitude to the silent mage, but he was preoccupied, already attending to the larger dragon.

Chapter 36

653 OM Tarandeer
Year of the Leaping Rabbit

Norman's Tower

Peter was glad to be back at the tower, away from the books and sitting indoors for days at a time. For two weeks he'd been holding all his boyishness inside with barely any chance to stretch his legs. The first thing he had done was jump off the cart and run for the tools his mother had given him, that he hadn't had a chance to pull out and use yet.

He knew exactly what his first project would be.

In Bakar, he had seen things that were foreign to Pugton. He had seen the gutters that people used to run rainwater down to barrels. He had seen the water wheels that were used along the river to run mills. He had seen the winches used for hanging wet clothing across the street. In his mind's eye, he pictured a vast system for carrying water from the small stream. It would branch at need, up to the second storey kitchen, along to the vegetable patch, over to a tub for cleaning clothes. Anywhere he needed water to go, he could get it there with minimal effort.

Every spare moment he had over the next two weeks became devoted to his great project, cutting down trees to carve buckets, stripping long sections of bark for guttering, gathering grass to dry and turn into twine. He took as much time out to do this as possible—he found he had little in common with the visiting apprentice, who was a 17-year-old girl who complained at being stuck in a backwoods where bugs and dirt were, apparently, 'everywhere' and where the food 'tasted weird' and who was not at all interested in discussing anything with a ten-year-old boy.

Searching for the raw materials gave him a delightful soreness in his muscles as he pushed himself to the limit of his young body. He felt like he became stronger with each tree he felled and dragged back to the tower, which encouraged him to fell more mature trees with more suitably wide trunks.

Working with the wood made him feel as if the world disappeared. Each of the tools his mother had passed along to him had purpose that he discovered from the way it fit into his hand and the way it worked the wood. Each day was spent running guttering overhead, each evening spent carving buckets to transport the water up to the guttering, and each night he rolled into bed happily and slept soundly.

Every time he stalled, he would pull out the small ceramic ring that Scaramond had given him, flipping it over and wondering what the secrets were that the mage had hinted at. He remembered that little balcony each time he pulled the ceramic ring out, and just the memory would relax him until he was rocking in time with the waves in his head. Each time, insight would shortly follow, until he started to consider the flat ring lucky. By the end of the fourth day, he repurposed some of his grass twine into a lanyard so that the ring would remain next to his skin at all times.

He finished the system a single day before he was due to go to Jerros, and after gazing at his marvellous water carrier for some time, he stepped out to visit the alarm frogs one more time. He hadn't visited them at all since their return from Bakar and he felt as if he were ignoring friends. After some time amongst their number, he sat down on a fallen log and pulled out the flat ceramic ring from around his neck.

The relaxation came on swiftly, and he could hear the sea once more. With time to spend on looking at the ring rather than building a water carrier, he was able to focus on the ring itself. It looked like nothing much, he thought. There was no patterning, no markings. He focussed on the hole in the centre, wondering what it was for (other than hanging on a lanyard).

A movement in his peripheral vision made him look up, and there before him was a glass doorway. A doorway that led to a balcony. A balcony that looked out onto the ocean. On the balcony was a small cast iron seat and table, and on the table was a note held down by a stone.

The sound of the waves was louder now, especially when Peter reached out to open the door and step through. He lifted the note from the table.

> *Peter,*
>
> *The sea fills you, so I offer you this trinket. The balcony stands over a spot in the southern seas, far west of Delingaard. No ships travel these waters. Here you can be secure and alone.*
>
> *The portal door will open and close when you focus on the space in the middle of the token. It will only open accidentally once. In the future, it will require intent to open for you. I recommend being careful with who you show this portal to. Such things are often looked upon with envy, and I would not wish this stolen from you.*
>
> *So long as the token is with you, the sea remains with you. You don't need the portal to be open to access the energy of these waves. Keep it with you.*
>
> *Scaramond.*

Chapter 37

1 OM Linter

The Year of True Sight

Atinien Mountain

The way up the stairs felt even further than the way down, but Norman was determined not to take shortcuts on this journey. If a wizard of more than 700 years could make this climb on a regular basis, so could he.

Scaramond was still there, a few paces behind, stopping only when Norman stopped and seeming never to tire. There was no conversation, just the somewhat unnerving presence of the other man. It felt somehow wrong to break that hallow quietude and so Norman made no attempt to break it. At times the silence was so profound that he felt as if he were deaf, and in those moments he would lift a hand to his ear and press on the tragus, just to hear the scraping of skin-on-skin and the change in resonance.

No stairway is eternal, and eventually the quality of the air changed — perhaps an imperceptible freshness or change in temperature — to indicate that Albert's quarters were ahead.

Norman cleared his throat to ask the question that had plagued him each step. "So what now?"

"That depends on you, I suppose. My suggestion is that you need to get back to your apprentice. His birthday has to be close?"

"Tomorrow, actually," affirmed Norman.

"So close up the lodge, close up the mountain entrance, take the succession box, and go home. Seems simple enough to me."

"And the rest of it? I don't know how to be a Magus."

"You don't need to worry about any of that for today, nor for tomorrow. You are allowed a period of grace. When you are ready, you will open the succession box and, I am led to believe, find a book that carries the notes from each previous Magus."

Exhausted by the events of the past two days, Norman just nodded in response.

"I'll help you get packed away, then I'll get you home. I can only imagine how much of a toll these past days have placed on you."

Again, Norman just nodded in response as he rose the final steps of the long climb, heavy legs, heavy head, heavy heart.

Chapter 38

1 OM Linter
The Year of True Sight

Norman's Tower

True to his word, Scaramond transported Norman home, directly to his bedroom.

The portal ring still shone in the centre of the room, less heat than before but continuing to sizzle and fill the room with light.

Norman could not find it in himself to care about the ring right now — fatigue had taken over and he could barely hold his eyes open. Scaramond directed him to his bed, then tucked him in as if he were a child.

"The box is here by the head of your bed. I'll stay, just for tonight, to make certain you're okay in the morning. Get some sleep."

"Wait," Norman mumbled, fishing around in his pocket. He pulled out the silver coin. "Please give this to Petunia. Tell her I'm sorry for taking it."

Scaramond took the tiny coin reverently. "I will. Sleep now. Everything else can wait."

The second floor was filled with chatter that suddenly

stopped as Scaramond descended. Petunia was the first to recover from the surprise, and she zipped over to him, flying in loops and swirls that showed off her happiness.

"Scaramond! I found my mother," the tiny dragon gushed at him. "Chance is here, and Suzie, and Peter, and me, and now Misty!" This was followed by clicks, creaks and whistles, and Peter felt a pang of jealousy at the obvious communication that he couldn't understand.

A big smile creased Scaramond's face at the dragon's words. "And I have found another thing of yours, little blossom," he said to the dragon, holding out her coin. "Norman needed to borrow it, just for a little bit. Now I would very much like to meet your mother. And of course I would be honoured to give her a home until she wishes to seek out her own lodgings."

Petunia grabbed at the coin, her acquisitiveness taking forefront in her mind.

Misty stepped out from behind the table, which had mostly hidden her from Scaramond's sight. His face dropped as he saw her state, and he rushed forward, clicking, groaning and squealing in an approximation of the noises Peter had just heard from Petunia.

"No need to fret, Scarred One," Misty said in the garbled voice caused by her bluntened tongue. "The young wizard here showed me respect in removing my wings as quickly as he could, laying on hands to stem the flow of my vital fluids. The healing he provided still courses through me."

Peter started. "Healing? I didn't do anything."

Misty turned her head to look at him. "You have no need for modesty. The magic you wield is powerful. I thank you for its gift."

"But I can't use my magic. It doesn't work." Peter looked to Scaramond. "Tell her. You can see magic. You can look and see."

A small smile played across Scaramond's face as he duly pricked the flesh between two of his fingers with the long hatpin he wore, frost covering his eyes.

"Let's see here." He stepped over to the window. "I see that you've made this fantastic water-carrying device. It plays rather loose with the concept of gravity, doesn't it?" He ran his hands along the stonework on the wall. "The gaps in the stone should be quite drafty. I can't imagine how Norman managed before you came along." He stepped up to Peter and ran a finger along the edge of his linen tunic. "This tunic looks like the one you were wearing that first day I met you. You were just ten at the time, and quite a bit smaller than you are now. You know, I do believe it may be the same tunic." He ran his fingers over his pin. "And it's strange how I never have to sharpen this pin, don't you think?"

Peter swallowed heavily. "So… is this all me?"

Scaramond lay a hand on Peter's shoulder. "It's all you. Always has been. And I think you can add healing to the list of things you do without intending to. Just keep doing what you do." Scaramond tapped the head of his pin against his lips in thought. "You become a journeyman tomorrow, at which point you'll be free to make your own employment decisions. I would like to offer you a place in my tower as my research companion. I'll not place limitations on that—so long as you're happy to remain, I'm happy to pay for your services. You'll get a safe environment to test what you can do, and I'll get someone who can help gather ingredients and test reagents. Then when Chance finishes his apprenticeship in a few months, you can decide whether you want to stay or set out with him. No need to decide today of course. Give it a good think. If you like the idea, we can discuss remuneration."

Peter's head swam. He had thought his magic impotent. Norman had not broached the subject of further employment, so the idea of moving to Bakar was something to consider. He wouldn't want to leave Petunia behind, but perhaps she would come with him. And Mum. What would Mum do? He was looking forward to time with her.

Leaving the others to chat, he excused himself so he could lose himself in chores.

Chapter 39

HAPPY BIRTHDAY

1 OM Linter
The Year of True Sight

Norman's Tower

On the morning of Peter's eighteenth birthday, everything seemed almost normal again. Not wishing to intrude, Scaramond and Chance had gone for an early morning hike (Scaramond seemed excited to show Chance the "delightful amphibious warbling" of the alarm frogs). Misty had claimed a spot on the second floor as her own and was spending a lot of her time sleeping, curled up in a way that her body had not had a chance to in many years. Norman was back where he belonged, if sadder and bowed down like the world depended upon him alone. Petunia — having found a new, much more secretive location, for her hoard — was now curled up on Peter's shoulder, and Suzie sat, silent and still, sunning herself at the front stairs as Felicity made her entrance.

Far from being on-foot like she had arrived all those years ago, she made her way in a two-horse carriage, driven by a chauffeur, and decked out in fine brocade and lace. No longer skin and bone, the years had added fat to her frame and her plump face reddened and sweated in the morning sun.

"Ooh, there's my little boy," she crooned as he approached,

and she bustled forward to squeeze his cheeks between her hands. "It's your big day!"

Norman walked up silently between the two. "Yes, today will be quite the ordeal," he said gravely. "I do hope you've brought Peter's earnings — it's quite important..."

"Yes, yes," Felicity said, tapping the side of the carriage. "The chest is in here, as per the instructions that lump of stone vomited at me last week."

"Good," Norman said. "The contract will be triggered at the exact time of Peter's birth and will release him as a free agent into the world." He turned to Peter. "Once my mark is removed from your wrist, you will become fully responsible for the effects of your magic. You may find yourself getting whipped around by some backlash for a little while — I've been redirecting what flow there has been into my own system these past years so you didn't injure yourself, but you have the capacity to use good judgement now."

He reached into the carriage for the chest, then frowned as it moved easily.

"Are you sure it's all there?" he asked, "It feels light."

Felicity tutted. "Well, there were some expenses, but we can sort all that out later."

"How much," he asked quietly.

"I don't really know, but I'm sure we can total it up tomorrow. No more than a couple of thousand out, I'm sure. Peter doesn't mind, do you darling?"

Norman paled. "Peter doesn't mind? It's not up to him. Please tell me this is a joke."

Peter butted in, "It's okay, Mum's fine..."

Norman stopped him as Felicity said, "No, no joke. I've had expenses, you know. And of course, once you set me up in that tent, my social status changed. My previous customers dropped off because my house looked too fancy, and I picked up a higher class of clientele who had different expectations. I was expected to garb myself differently, wear different outfits every day, and put on dinner parties, and society requires attendance at all sorts of balls, you know. I needed new dresses for all of those. And I need to get my hair styled so that I'm at the height of fashion. And these things add up. But no need to worry—I'm going to sort it out..."

"This was a three-way contract!" Norman roared. "Magical contracts aren't something to fool with!" His hands grasped at his hair as he started to pace wildly. "There's time, there must be time," he muttered. "What time?" he shouted to Felicity. "What time was he born? How much time do we have to make up the shortfall?"

"Ooh, he's a morning baby, don't you recall? How do you forget that day? I can't be sure of the exact time—I was a little preoccupied, what with all that happened, but mid-morn. Should be coming up soon."

"Not enough time," Norman railed. "We can only hope for the grace of the universe. You need to give him the box. Now."

"Now? But we haven't even had cake yet!" Felicity complained obliviously. "Ooh, I feel a little dizzy."

"Now!" Norman yelled, frantic. He shoved the box into Felicity's hands and pulled Peter forward. "Grab it, boy, and pray."

Peter felt a tingling on his wrist as he grasped the box, golden light travelling from the sigil to the wooden casket. Then the light overflowed the box and started to travel up Felicity's arms.

"What's it... what's it doing?" she cried, "It, ow, it hurts. It pinches!"

Peter let go of the box, but the flow of light continued, engulfing Felicity's entire body as the box fell to the ground, golden coins scattering in a pile on the grass.

Petunia lifted into the sky, red wings fluttering in distress. "Why's it hurting her? What's going on?"

"The universe knows value. A value was sealed into the

contract. The universe is trying to meet the value that was owed from the party that failed to meet the terms." Norman said, feeling sick. "What have I done?" he muttered to himself, a wild look in his wide eyes.

Felicity had started emitting a high-pitched keen as her cheeks started to hollow. Her plump arms thinned, their ample softness becoming twig-like, skin clinging to bare bones.

Petunia's movements became frantic. She zipped around, saying "What do we do? What do we do?" Then she zipped off into the bushes.

"Is Mum going to die?" whispered Peter, sinking to his knees. He reached out with his silence, trying to stem the flow of magic around Felicity. The glow dimmed, the passage of magic slowed, but he feared he may have simply been prolonging the inevitable.

Tears streamed down Norman's face and a low moan issued from the depth of his chest as he watched Felicity's distress. "I'm sorry. I'm so sorry. For all of it. We're in a closed system. I can't help."

Felicity's keening faltered, becoming a wordless whistle as her clothing started to hang from her body, much too large for her shrunken frame.

Petunia flapped her way back, slower under the weight of her burden.

"Maybe you just need a little more," the tiny dragon cried, with little hope. "Just take this. Pay him more." And from her grasp, a single coin dropped into Felicity's open hand.

Felicity flopped to the ground, silent. Then, almost imperceptibly at first, the flow of golden light retreated as Petunia's coin lifted into the air and travelled, as if by some spectral hand, to the pile of other coins. With a soft clink, it fell onto the pile of shinier coins, itself a spark amongst the wizard's gold.

Felicity's form filled out once more, paler, less plump than before, but no longer skeletal. Her steady breathing reassured

Peter that she still lived, and that perhaps she would be alright.

Peter barely felt the soft weight that fell into his sleeve as Norman stepped forward to inspect the silver coin, wiping the tears from his face with a trembling hand.

"What is it?" Norman asked. "I… I don't understand. Nothing special, just a silver penny. A half-tarnished one at that."

Peter looked at Petunia. "You gave her your silver penny?" he asked, "We only just got it back. It meant everything to you! It's the last piece of your hoard you have left."

Petunia blinked. "Well, I had to do something."

A look of realisation crossed Norman's face. "Of course. It's not monetary value that gets measured, it's actual value. And a dragon's hoard… well, that's immeasurable!"

Peter cradled his mother's head in his arms. "You're okay, Mum. It's stopped and it's not going to happen again." He rocked her as if she were a child.

Running his hand down her arm, two large gold coins tumbled from his long sleeve. Norman bent to pick them up, then handed one to Peter.

"You'll need this," he grunted, flipping the other over in his fingers.

Peter peered at it, unable to think past the immediacy of the moment right now. "What is it? It doesn't look like any money that I'm familiar with."

Norman had to clear his throat a few times before he could speak, and his voice was almost a whisper when he finally managed to get around the constriction. "It's a contract token. You're a Journeyman mage now, not a Master yet, but you have the right to take an apprentice. One goes into your wrist for the duration of your study and two come out when it ends, one for the mage you were apprenticed to and one for you, so that you can bind an apprentice to yourself."

Peter looked at it with dull eyes. "So I can take an apprentice?" He looked at his mother, who was shaking in his arms. "So I can make a contract that has no conscience? That doesn't take people's lives into consideration? A contract that can kill someone just because of money? I don't want to ever make a contract like that. I don't ever want to hurt someone that makes a deal because they're poor. Is this real gold?"

"Yes," said Scaramond, who had walked silently up behind the group. "It's as real as it gets."

"Then it belongs to Petunia." He held the coin out to the small dragon. "Petunia doesn't have a hoard now, and I don't want her to ever be hungry, so this is hers."

Felicity looked up. Her face was stained with the salt from her tears, blotchy. Seeing Scaramond, she clutched at the front of her dress with trembling fingers, trying to make the too-loose garment fit a little better.

"Oh, a gentleman." She raised shaky fingers to try to right her hair. "I do apologise for the state of my appearance, it seems I've had a little accident."

"Not at all, milady. You are positively radiant and let nobody tell you otherwise." He offered her an arm as he used the other hand to subtly scratch himself on his pin. As she rose, the dress began to cling to her a little more securely, allowing her to relax. "Let me walk you inside where you can take a moment to gather yourself."

As the two moved slowly towards the tower, Peter spoke. "Scaramond?"

Scaramond turned, pausing their walk for a moment. "Yes?" he asked.

Peter responded firmly. "Yes."

Chapter 40

1 OM Linter
The Year of True Sight

Norman's Tower

Norman looked across at Peter.

"So, now that's done, it's time to think about the future. I would have asked this a couple of days ago, but things happened and I wasn't here. I'd like you to stay on. The bed in there is yours as long as you like. I'd continue to pay…"

Peter cut him off. "I've already taken up an offer of employment from Scaramond. I'll be setting out for Bakar with him when he leaves. I want to stay with Misty and make certain she's well, and he's got the facilities for my continued research into my abilities."

"Oh," said Norman. He took a deep breath. "I'll miss you, as I'm sure will Suzie and Petunia…"

Petunia came flitting over. "I heard my name! Peter, can you help me carry that big gold coin thing to Bakar with me? It's too heavy and my mother needs me. What if someone catches her again? I'd need to save her! It's a happy time when I save her, but it's sad before then."

"You're going too, Petunia? I didn't realise. It will be very quiet here without either of you." Norman felt his chin tremble and he blinked back tears. "Things will not be the same around here."

Suzie had been basking in the sun, but now stepped over, placing her head directly into Norman's hand. He stroked the rough, warm stone, thankful for the reassurance as Peter and Petunia walked away.

Scaramond was talking quietly to Felicity as Peter entered the tower.

"Oh, Peter," Felicity said, her voice stronger now that the nightmare had ended. "I've just been speaking to this gentleman here and he says you're to take up residence in Bakar. I was wondering, that house I live in. Can it fold back down into that little box again?"

"Yes, Mum. I can fold it back down. Why?"

"It's just… that's Norman's land and, after today, I'm not really sure I want to stay there. I don't want a reminder of the… oh, the… the money incident. Besides, without the stipend I was receiving from your apprenticeship, I'm not certain I can afford to stay in Pugton. But I could build a new clientele in a big place like Bakar, and Mister Mond here says he has land available that I could settle upon for a good rent—far less than I paid for that hovel we were in when you were a child. I would understand if you don't want me riding on your coattails, but I think…"

"I'd love to be able to spend time with you, Mum. I think it sounds splendid!"

Felicity's smile was large, even if her eyes were still somewhat haunted from the events of the morning.

"That's settled then. And it's still your birthday, but there's been no cake!"

Norman's slow trudge had brought him up the stairs just in time to hear the last. "Cake. Yes. I think I have something… somewhere…" He rummaged through his pockets, searching, then pulled out a small, pink-frosted fruit cake and placed it on the table. The frosting had slumped somewhat on one side, and the cake appeared slightly burned, but it was a cake.

"Sorry, the last few days have been somewhat strange. But happy birthday, Peter. I'm feeling rather tired now, so I'll be going upstairs. I may be some time. Don't wait around for me, I know you all have to get on the road soon."

With that, Norman continued his trudge up the stairs, Suzie silently following.

Chapter 41

1 OM Linter

The Year of True Sight

Norman's Tower

Scaramond was highly considerate of Felicity's hesitation around magic, Peter noted. The carriage driver had stayed out of the way the entire morning, sitting by the vegetable patch and nibbling on his pre-prepared lunch, and Scaramond had wittered him out, whispering in his ear about transportation of the entire carriage.

There were considerable logistics issues to discuss, it seemed, as the way would require passage for not one passenger, but six, one of those being a dragon who would take up one entire bench seat.

He was careful in arranging who sat where. Felicity and Chance sat along one padded seat, looking forward, Misty on the other seat as it did not matter which direction she was facing while travelling. The tiny Petunia took up barely any space, so she was free to flit about the cabin as she saw fit. The blinds were drawn, and Scaramond motioned for Peter to sit beside the driver's seat. Peter was slightly surprised when the driver mounted the footman's place at the back of the carriage and Scaramond the driver's seat, but all became clear when, just five minutes into the journey, Scaramond drew his pin from his lapel.

"You don't need to use that. I know you don't. And I don't like it when you hurt yourself," Peter murmured to the man next to him.

Scaramond simply put the pin away and, without stopping the carriage, opened a portal the likes of which amazed Peter. It covered the entire road, seamlessly connecting to the landscape a little outside of Pugton. The carriage drove through, and Peter considered that anyone inside looking out would barely notice the transition. A few minutes later they pulled up outside of Felicity's home, and with Chance's offered hand of assistance, she climbed out.

"My, that journey seemed so quick!" she said. "We were so deep in conversation that the time just flew by."

Scaramond smiled his close-mouthed smile and bowed slightly. "I am glad the way was pleasant for milady." Then he tipped the chauffeur, who nodded and touched the brim of his hat in respect, then trundled off towards the tavern.

"I've explained the situation to your chauffeur, milady. He informs me that the carriage is yours, not rented, so with your permission, we'll travel to Bakar in the same manner once we've finalised your accommodation requirements."

"Ooh, there are some dresses I haven't finished yet..."

Peter had anticipated this. "Have they been paid for yet, Mum? You used to take payment only after the dress had been finished."

"No, I still work it the same way."

"Then it doesn't matter that they're not finished. You can make them display pieces in Bakar when you set up your shop. Show new customers the quality of your work. And I think you should charge more. Triple your prices."

Felicity stared at her son. "Triple my prices?"

Scaramond placed a gentle hand on Felicity's forearm. "Your son is being conservative. Ever has it been that expense makes a product more desirable. Those with money will flock to your service if you place a high value on it. Ten times the price would be my recommendation."

Felicity blushed. "If you think so…"

"I certainly do. And you should be taking at least half of the payment up front for commissions. But we can talk accounting later. Have you anything that needs to be moved inside before we fold up your pavilion?"

There was nothing, so Peter immediately lifted the doormat, which triggered the entire pavilion to fold up into a small cube once more. Felicity averted her eyes during this process, and refused to look at the blank area of dirt that her home had once occupied. She climbed back into the carriage, saying that Petunia and Misty would be getting lonely without her, all without acknowledging that anything untoward had occurred.

Troubled, Peter grabbed the cube and climbed back into the seat he had filled previously. As Scaramond and Chance also took their places, Peter murmured his concerns to Scaramond.

"Mum seems really averse to magic now. Bakar's a six-hour journey. It's going to really upset her if it's only ten minutes like the trip from the tower to here."

"Not to worry. We'll set off. She'll be asleep before we portal, and she can remain so until tonight. It will seem as if she slept the entire journey and that no magic occurred."

Five minutes later they portalled to Bakar, directly into the grounds of Scaramond's tower. True to his word, Felicity was asleep, so while Chance and Peter found a quiet nook to commune with each other, Scaramond organised accommodations for Misty and Petunia, who wanted to lodge together.

"Petunia will need her gold," Peter called after the Scaramond.

He turned back to Peter. "You're really giving up your

option to pass along your skills?"

"No," Peter said. "I just don't need a contract to do it. There's really no need to take children away from their families. Completely unnecessary. And I don't see why they need to be trained one at a time. It seems wasteful. I can understand if it's dangerous for a child with an unpredictable sense trigger to stay with family, but we should have schools."

A faint smile tugged on Scaramond's face. "Really? That's interesting. I think I can help with that. This estate used to be a school. Most of it's just been dimensionally hidden. After all, what use is a library like mine if there's nobody to use it? I could dust off the old facilities. We'll talk." He took the token from Peter's outstretched hand. "Petunia will get it immediately."

Six hours later, Peter and Scaramond drove the carriage to Felicity's new address, a space surprisingly close to the main thoroughfares of town. Peter threw down the cube, which opened into a bright pavilion once more, and together they woke Felicity.

"We're here, Mum. You were sleeping so soundly that we decided to drop off Chance and the dragons before bringing you to your new home. It's set up and ready."

Bleary eyed, Felicity yawned. "We're here? I slept the entire way. Best sleep I've had in ages."

With a hand either side, she stepped down from the carriage. "It seems all good. Can one of you put the horses in the stable around the back? I haven't eaten since that bit of burnt cake at Norman's. Would you like to join me?"

"No, Mum. You get yourself settled. I'll be back in the morning to show you around."

The horses stabled, the carriage put away, the two mages strolled in the clear evening air, returning to Scaramond's estate.

"So, about that school..."

Epilogue

4 OM Barduce
The Year of Thrown Heretics

Merethin

Argentus Barduce paced in front of the slender mage with a thunderous look on his face. "Once again it's your bloody school. It's the fourth attempt this month and I am NOT seeing the positive side of this like you keep trying to tell me."

"It's not any of the staff. They've all been thoroughly vetted by mind-mages and found to be either politically passive or they lean towards you. It must be the students themselves. They congregate in their halls at night and plot these assassination attempts together."

"So you say." The muscled warrior stared the school-keeper down. "I don't stay Magus by believing every bureaucrat that simpers in front of me. You will shut the school down, effective immediately. I won't have these pockets of influence swaying the next generation."

"Yes, Magus. I was anticipating this turn of events, and I have a solution for the problem." The thin mage drew a large gold coin out of his pocket. "With this token, a mage can bind an apprentice to him. The mage is expected to pay a wage to the apprentice, to be held aside by a third party. The token seals all three into a contract with rather unpleasant effects for reneging in any way."

"Interesting. How do you see this being applied?"

"Rather than the schools, we hand these out to mages that we have vetted thoroughly. Each mage takes a child as apprentice. The child is removed from the family home and any heretical opinions the family unit may be harbouring. We bind the mage, the apprentice, and the family with strong ties of obligation to your leadership."

The Magus stopped pacing and settled his large frame into the ornately carved throne behind him.

"This seems an acceptable direction for the short term. But what of the long term? I intend to be in this seat for a long time. Children grow quickly."

"That's a beautiful thing about these tokens. On the apprentice's birthday, a second token is created — one for the Master, one for the Journeyman — and at this juncture, the adherence to your leadership has been assured. The next generation is encouraged to go out and take apprentices of their own. No more pockets for dissention to arise. No huddles of teens plotting foment. Especially if you take the time while handing tokens out to weed out the undesirables."

Argentus leaned back in the throne, a large smile on his face. "I approve your plan, Scaramond. And now that you're going to have more time on your hands, let's see what you can put together to ensure smooth succession..."

Appendix

OM Fellin (24 years)

Interregnum (4 years)

         (This period is sometimes termed the Interregnum war or the Highmage war)

OM Barduce (973 years)

4   Contract tokens replace school system

         The succession box is created

OM Jlaskil (526 years)

OM Houn (1438 years)

OM Daraskell (1947 years)

OM Pitchworth (842 years)

OM Tarandeer

1   Albert Tarandeer becomes Magus, age 78

619   Norman Linter is born

621   Gareth Diefen is born

624   Felicity Parnat is born

627   Norman Linter enters the employ of Albert Tarandeer, age 8

637   Norman Linter reaches majority

642   Felicity Parnat weds Gareth Diefen

643   Death of Gareth Diefen

         Peter Diefen is born

653   Misty enters household of the Cutler family

         Petunia is hatched

         Peter Diefen enters the employ of Norman Linter, age 10

661   Misty is rescued from enslavement

1	Death of Albert Tarandeer
	Norman Linter becomes Highmage and Magus, age 44
	Peter Diefen reaches majority

Abercrombie	A Highmage
Albert Tarandeer	Norman's mentor Magus
Bellamy Foljur	A Highmage
Brian	Part of Reginald's retinue
Calder Wainwright	Mayor of Pugton
Chance	Scaramond's apprentice Vocal focus
Dagney Dunforth	Known as "Dingy" Dunforth. Rich landowner in the Pugton region known for gambling.
Felicity Diefen	Peter's mother.
Gantry	A mage, familiar with stone magic
Gareth Diefen	Mage with architectural focus. Peter's father Felicity's husband Norman's friend Apprentice to Theophrastus
Mick	Enforcer to Dagney Dunforth
Misty	Dragon—gold Full name—*The Sun Shines on the Misty Valleys and Burns Away the Shadow* Petunia's mother Enslaved by the Cutler family between 653—661 OM Tarandeer
Norman Linter	Mage with scent focus. Apprentice to Albert Tarandeer Peter's mentor Friend to Gareth Diefen

	Magus
Peter Diefen	Apprentice to Norman Linter
Petunia	Dragon — red
	Full name — *The Blossom of the One Who Offers Life*
	Misty's daughter
Pimply Boy	Part of Reginald's retinue
Reginald Cutler	The butcher's son. Known as a bully in the local Pugton area
Scaramond	A mage with a pain focus.
	Mentor to Chance
	Known as the 'Scarred One'
Skinny Boy	Part of Reginald's retinue
Suzie	Gargoyle in the shape of a cat, companion to Norman Linter.
Theophrastus	A Highmage. Shapechanger.

Alarm-frogs	Magical frogs that emit piercing shrieks if disturbed
Alven	Intelligent marsupials that inhabit the Northeastern Reaches. The Alven are highly communal and exist in small clans that trade with each other.
Atinien Mountain	A mountain in Varthien's Northern Reach, home to Magus Albert Tarandeer
Bakar	An unwalled town of roughly 10,000 people.
Chirren	Intelligent arthropods. The Chirren are semi-aquatic social creatures that populate littoral zones across most of Varthien.
Delingaard	A country in the south-west of Varthien's western continent
Delingaard Imperial Palace	Imperial palace of the Delingaard line, a family known for liberal views on slavery and torture.
Fire Starter	A magical device that sets a small twig on fire for the purpose of firing hearths
Gargoyle	A magical creature created from artistic inspiration
Garthanian	A forest in the southern part of the Eastern Continent, known for a species of tree that can communicate with other living organisms.
Glisterweed	A light-emitting plant found in underground caverns
Hedgemage	A person whose magic requires active application of plants or minerals.

Highmage	A mage who has been appointed to the Council of Mages
Light-bob	A magical light which can be set to stay in one place or follow a given subject.
Mage	A person who is able to use magic
Magus	The thirteenth member of the Council of Mages, who stands apart from the rest of the council and is the arbiter of disputes. Often seen as the leader of the Council. Can set policy.
OM	"Our Magus"; terminology to describe the year, marking from the year of ascension to the year of the Magus stepping down. Years where no magus sits are marked as interregnum.
Pugton	Birthplace of Peter Diefen. Home of Felicity Diefen.
Sense Trigger	A focus that enables a mage to cast a spell. Sense triggers differ person to person.
Sorcerer	A person whose magic requires active application of schematics or mathematics.
Storyhoard	A dragon who collects the stories of other dragons, to pass along to future generations of dragon.
Succession box	In the wake of the sudden death of Magus Fellin and the 4 year interregnum that followed, the succession box was created in 4 OM Barduce by Magus Argentus Barduce to remove issues arising from the death of any Highmage.
Varthien	The world in which the events take place
Wizard	A mage who has learned to use magic without relying upon a sense trigger
Wyrm	A dragon

Wyrmling   An infant dragon